STAND

AT

FOSTERS

FIELD

a novella

Brian J Anderson

All rights reserved.
This book is a work of fiction. Names, characters, businesses, organizations, places, events and incidents either are the product of the author's imagination or are used fictitiously. Any resemblance to actual persons, living or dead, events or locales is entirely coincidental.
ISBN-13: 978-1523244133
Copyright © 2016 Brian J. Anderson

Also by Brian J. Anderson

The Ascent of PJ Marshall
Ghosts of Florence Pass

For exclusive access to Brian J. Anderson's latest work in progress, along with information about author promotions, giveaways and contests, visit bjandersonauthor.com.

For Beth.

Love you, babe.

The author wishes to acknowledge Rebecca Powers for her help in bringing this book to life.

"Thistle and Weeds" and "Dust Bowl Dance" by Mumford and Sons were the spark and the fuel that got this story cooking.

Thank you all.

PART 1

How the Boars Fit In

ON the last day of ninth grade Jacob Miller was leaving school and when he went outside he became very excited because he saw Angie Swenson by the bike racks and she was by herself unlocking her bike. Jacob was excited because he had wanted to talk to Angie for a long time but he hadn't been able to summon the courage to do it. He hadn't been able to talk to her not because he was intimidated by her nor was it because he was intimidated by girls in general. He hadn't talked to Angie Swenson because of her brother Mark Swenson. But now school was over and Jacob didn't know when he would see her again and he really didn't care about her brother right now. Jacob had taken his bike to school as well so he put his backpack on the ground and turned the numbers on the combination lock securing his bike to the rack and then he unlatched the lock and put it in his backpack with the chain and as he was doing these things he looked at Angie Swenson.

What're you doing this summer, Jacob said.

What?

I said what're you doing this summer.

Angie was turning the cable around the seat post of her bike to store it and as she did this she was looking around the parking lot and down the sidewalk and behind her as if beset by demons. She secured the cable ends with the lock and looked at Jacob and said I don't know.

He's not here, Jacob said.

What?

Mark's not here. I checked.

Angie didn't say anything and she put her backpack on and pulled the front tire of her bike from the rack.

What's the deal with him anyway, Jacob said.

Angie was rolling her bike across the sidewalk to the road so Jacob pulled his own bike from the rack and followed her.

Nothing, Angie said. Don't follow me okay?

I just want to talk to you, Jacob said. I'm not trying to be a jerk or anything.

Angie rolled her bike off the curb and into the road and stepped over the bar. She looked at Jacob who was standing on the sidewalk holding his bike.

I know you're not, she said. But you can't.

Can't what?

Talk to me.

Why can't you talk to people?

I can talk to people.

Why can't you talk to people at school?

Angie put one foot on the pedal of her bike and the other foot she put on the curb to steady herself and then she put on her helmet.

I have to go, she said.

Jacob.

What?

My name's Jacob.

I know, she said.

Is it because you can't talk to me or because you don't want to, Jacob said.

Angie looked at him through her hair that had been

pushed down over her eyes by the bike helmet. She tucked it up inside and turned and rose on the pedals and onto the seat.

I can't, she said.

I have a treehouse in the Fosters' back woods, Jacob said. It's actually my dad's deer stand but I pimped it out. I stay overnight there sometimes. It's off the park road by the tower.

I know where it is, Angie said.

Jacob thought about this. He didn't know how she knew where the stand was but right now it didn't matter because she was still talking to him and maybe she liked him because she knew his name and that he had a treehouse and because she knew where it was.

Okay, Jacob said. If you want to talk sometime I'll be there most nights.

Angie looked at him again and Jacob thought she smiled a little bit but he couldn't be sure and then she turned and rode away.

* * *

It was the middle of July and Jacob hadn't seen Angie Swenson at the stand or in town or at the lake or anywhere. He was in the back yard with his father digging out the stump of a maple tree that had fallen during a thunderstorm the week before and he asked his father what he knew about the Swenson family.

Why do you want to know, Jacob's father said.

Jacob shrugged and said just curious I guess.

Well I don't know a whole lot, Jacob's father said. Dale's pretty well off on account of Mary coming from Texas oil.

When did she die, Jacob said.

Jacob's father thought about this for a moment as he worked.

Guess it's been ten fifteen years, he said. Dale took Mark out of school a couple years back to work the acres they've got up towards Benton. I don't see much of Dale anymore but Mark shows up at the co-op fairly regular for parts and repairs and whatnot. Not sure about the girl.

She's in my grade, Jacob said.

That right?

Yeah.

How's she seem?

She seems sad.

That sounds right.

I think she's lonely too.

Jacob's father didn't say anything.

I tried talking to her once, Jacob said.

Jacob's father had been prying at the stump with his shovel but now he stopped working and stood the shovel on the ground and held it there looking at Jacob.

Tried to?

Yeah.

About what?

Nothing. Just trying to be friendly.

She say anything?

Not really.

And was that the end of it?

Yeah.

Jacob's father nodded and took up the shovel and went on with his work.

I'd be real careful about doing that Jacob.

Now Jacob stopped digging and prying at the stump and put up his shovel.

What do they do to her?

Jacob's father looked at Jacob but didn't stop working.

What have you heard, he said.

Just that they're real mean to her. And that they won't let her talk to anyone. I heard when Bobby Cramer asked her to come out to the lake once Mark found out and cut him with a mower blade.

The handle of the shovel Jacob's father was using to pry and dig at the stump made a cracking sound when he was prying with it and Jacob's father cursed and turned it in his hands and looked at it. He stood it on the ground and shook his head and looked at Jacob.

I suppose that's all true enough, he said. But I reckon they're more than just mean to her.

Jacob thought about this and said what do you mean.

I think you know what I mean. I don't have to say it.

Jacob thought about this for some time just standing there and holding his shovel and watching his father bend his own shovel over his knee to test its strength where it had cracked.

That's not right, Jacob said.

I know it's not.

They can't do that. Someone should do something.

What should they do, Jacob's father said.

Tell the sheriff. Put them in jail.

Jacob's father shook his head and took Jacob's shovel and turned and walked to the garage and Jacob followed.

The sheriff knows, Jacob's father said. If I know and Bob

Wilkins and Gary Schroeder down at the co-op know then the sheriff knows.

Jacob's father put Jacob's shovel up on the rack and then he set his own shovel on the workbench and took a roll of electrical tape from a nail on the wall and began to wrap the splintered handle of the shovel with it.

Unless there's charges brought there's not much he can do, Jacob's father said. It seems to me she doesn't want to do that.

She's scared of them, Jacob said.

Jacob's father thought about this and said that very well may be but the sheriff can't just put people in jail. It's more complicated than that.

No it's not, Jacob said.

Jacob's father looked at him and then breathed out with a heavy sigh and then cut the electrical tape and pressed the cut end down onto the handle and put the roll of tape back on the nail.

You going out to the stand tonight, Jacob's father said.

Yeah.

You staying the night?

Probably.

Dan Foster says there's a boar been tearing up his beans out that way. Take my twelve gauge and if you see it take care of it for him.

Okay.

I'm going inside to call Pete over at O'Malley's. See if he can bring his grinder for that stump.

Okay.

Clean up the rest of our stuff out back and get washed for supper.

Jacob wanted to say more to his father about Angie Swenson and how her brother and father shouldn't treat her like that and that if the sheriff wasn't going to do something about it then someone else should but he didn't say anything.

* * *

After supper Jacob's father put his shotgun in its case and gave it to Jacob along with a box of shells which Jacob put in his backpack.

Remember I need you at the co-op tomorrow after dinner, Jacob's father said.

I know.

Jacob went to the garage and secured the gun case across the handlebars of his bike with bungee cord and then he put on his pack and rode slowly through town to guard against losing his balance with the awkward load. At the Kwik Trip he saw Mr. Foster who was filling his truck with gas and Jacob waved and Mr. Foster waved back.

You get that hog for me Jacob and I'll give your mother the ham for your Christmas dinner, Mr. Foster said.

They both laughed as Jacob rode past and Jacob said he'd do his best.

At the edge of town Jacob turned onto the gravel road separating the Fosters' back lot and Indian Lake Park which was a county park with a lot of deer that would come across to Mr. Foster's land to eat corn or beans. The deer from the park would get really big from eating corn and beans and since Mr. Foster didn't like the deer eating his crops and since there was no hunting allowed in the park Jacob's father had asked Mr. Foster if he could put a deer stand on his land to which Mr. Foster said of course.

When Jacob got to the trail leading to the stand he walked his bike up the trail for a little while and then leaned it against a tree. He took the gun case from the handlebars of his bike and put it over his shoulder and walked to the stand which was up the hill in an oak tree near the edge of Mr. Foster's soybean field. He set down the gun and his pack at the base of the tree and went to the field and looked around.

Since it was starting to get dark there were a lot of deer near the edges of Mr. Foster's field and when the deer heard Jacob walking to the field they raised their heads and looked at him but after a little while they must have decided Jacob wasn't a threat so they went back to eating beans. Jacob thought that Mr. Foster probably wouldn't mind if he shot some of the deer along with the boar that was eating his crops but he thought that the game warden would probably see things differently. Jacob looked along the tree line at the near edge of the field and he could see in several places where the rows of beans had been pulled from the ground and scattered and even the ground itself had been turned over and trampled as if by an army of men.

Jacob walked back into the woods to the stand and then he got to his knees and started to dig in the leaves and forest duff around him. He found the long piece of quarter round molding that he used to put up the rope ladder and bring it down and it had a bent nail in one end that he used to place the ladder parts over the branch and out of reach. He brought the ladder down and leaned the quarter round against the tree and picked up the shotgun and carried it up the ladder. He pushed the hatch up so that it tipped over on its hinge and fell onto the floor above his head and raised a cloud of dust that filled the stand and drifted down through the opening in the floor. Jacob reached up and set the gun on the floor and then went back down to get his pack and when he had everything inside he closed the hatch and sat with his back against the tree.

He sat there for a while without moving just resting and listening not for anything in particular but just listening. He thought about Angie Swenson and he wondered what was happening to her right then and he wondered whether they had a schedule for what they did to her or if they just decided they wanted to do it and then did it. He also thought about what his father had said about things being complicated and how the sheriff can't just arrest people. Jacob thought about that for a while and he decided that if he was the sheriff and he knew that something like that was going on he wouldn't think twice about it he would just walk up and arrest them. Then he thought about how he might just say screw it and not bother with arresting them and just shoot them. He didn't think it was complicated at all.

Jacob got up and opened the plywood box in the corner of the stand and the lid for the box was covered with plastic sheeting that was stapled under the edges to protect the contents of the box from the weather and he took out his sleeping pad and sleeping bag and unrolled them on the floor. He took the flashlight out of the box as well and put it on his sleeping bag but he left the blue plastic tarp folded up in the box since it looked like it was going to be a clear night and he didn't think he needed to tie it up against the weather. It was getting too dark to use the gun to hunt for boars he thought so he put it into the box along with the shells his father had sent with him and then he closed the box and picked up the flashlight and lifted the hatch and climbed down the ladder.

Jacob walked down the trail and across the gravel road and through the woods on the other side to the observation tower that was at the end of a spur trail in the park. He climbed the stairs to the top of the tower and looked through the telescope that was mounted on the railing for observing the landscape and he turned it so he could see the beach on the far side of the lake. The telescope wasn't very powerful and the light was gone but Jacob could make out the kids that were on the beach by the light of their bonfire. Indian Bluff was behind the beach and it towered over the beach to such a height that the kids and their cars and the bonfire all looked like miniatures in a model train set.

There were always kids from school there on summer nights swimming and dipping cups into a plastic barrel that was filled with a mixture of juice or soda and whatever kind of alcohol they could get. Sometimes the sheriff would come and the kids would tip the barrel over into the lake and dump the contents of their cups before he could walk down to the water but of course the sheriff knew what was going on and the kids knew that the sheriff knew but as long as nobody was hurting anyone else the sheriff just sent the kids home when he came.

Jacob saw his friend David West by the fire talking with Samantha Hicks who was Jacob's old girlfriend. Jacob smiled a little because David wasn't very good at talking to girls and the only time he really did was when he was drinking from a barrel. It seemed like David had been drinking from the barrel for some time because he was very animated in his speech and Samantha was smiling and laughing with him and every now and then they would embrace and one time even kissed.

David you dog, Jacob said.

As he looked through the telescope at the kids he knew from school he started to get excited because he was thinking about the time Samantha had used her hand to masturbate him after the game against Benton last year and also because he was watching Amy Shields and Megan Tanner run in and out of the water laughing in their bikinis. He thought about masturbating himself right there on the tower and he had even unzipped his pants but then he thought about Angie Swenson and decided not to. He wasn't thinking about what her father and brother did to her and that he shouldn't be thinking about sex because of it but he just didn't really care about sex as much when he thought about her. He thought that if she was there on the tower with him the idea of sex wouldn't even occur to him and they would just talk.

Jacob zipped up his pants and then he turned on the flashlight and pointed it at the beach and waved it around as he looked through the telescope. Megan Tanner saw the light when she was running into the lake and she stopped and waved at it and then she called to the others on the beach and then pretty soon everyone was waving. Jacob could hear them in the distance yelling his name and he saw that his friend David was motioning for him to come down to the beach but Jacob said no by waving the flashlight from side to side. When Jacob did this David gave him the finger and then turned around and lowered his swim trunks and mooned Jacob from the beach. Some of the other kids did this as well and Amy Shields even lifted her bikini top to show Jacob her breasts but she did this almost every time there was a party on the beach so it wasn't that unusual. Jacob thought that even though it wasn't unusual for Amy Shields to show her breasts it was still exciting and then he thought that maybe he would masturbate himself on the tower after all.

* * *

Jacob woke up early the next morning because there were wild boars in Mr. Foster's soybeans and they were grunting and snorting and fighting even though there were plenty of beans for them to share. He got out of his sleeping bag and stood up and looked out through the trees and because the light was weak he could barely make out the shapes of the boars digging and rooting at the edge of the field. There were three of them there and Jacob didn't think even if he got close enough to them he could get all three but like he told Mr. Foster he would do his best. Jacob opened the plywood box and took out the gun case and then took the gun out of it and opened the barrel and took three shells from the box and loaded them. When he looked up the boars were still eating and digging and were oblivious to his presence so Jacob cycled the first shell and put on his boots and lifted the hatch and set it down on the floor and climbed down the ladder.

When he got to the ground he walked slowly and used the trees that were between him and the boars as cover by ducking behind them and waiting in case they caught his scent and were watching out of the corners of their eyes. He didn't know if boars watched things out of the corners of their eyes but he wasn't taking any chances. Near the edge of the woods was a big walnut tree and when he got behind it he knew that was as far as he could go without exposing himself and so he got to one knee. The boars were still digging and chewing and stomping Mr.

Foster's bean plants but now Jacob was much closer to them and he could smell them and they smelled like turned eggs because they were farting as they rolled on the ground and they also smelled like mud and rot. Jacob thought about how he liked most kinds of animals and how most of them served some kind of purpose in the circle of things but he didn't like boars very much and maybe it was because he didn't know what purpose they served or in what way they fit into the circle.

Two of the boars started to fight and Jacob used the distraction to take the safety off the gun and shoulder it and swing the barrel around the side of the tree. The boars that were fighting were running away from him as they fought and they were lowering their heads and then tossing them back to try and catch each other's undersides with their tusks. Jacob watched them as they made a wide arc over the field and came back to where the third boar was still eating and digging with its snout.

When the boars that had been fighting stopped they were tired and panting and one of them was standing broadside to Jacob's tree so he shot it in the side behind its shoulder and it dropped to the ground and didn't move. When the other boars heard the shot they ran away from Jacob across the field and their legs were a blur and dust and plant matter flew from their hides as they ran. Jacob cycled another shell and he stood up and fired and he hit the boar that was closer to him in its rear leg and the leg shattered in the middle and swung underneath the boar on a tether of tissue and then the boar fell. The boar was thrashing on the ground and screaming and snorting when Jacob reached the place where it fell. It got up on its remaining legs and was starting to limp away but Jacob shot it in the side like he did with the first boar and it fell dead.

Jacob stood there for some time looking at the dead boar and his heart was beating fast and then he looked up to see if he could find the third boar but he couldn't. He looked down at the dead boar at his feet and then at the one dead by the edge of the woods and he wondered if Mr. Foster was serious about saving the hams for Christmas dinner. It had sounded like a joke at the time but now he wasn't sure. Jacob thought about maybe taking their entrails out just in case but then decided that it was a joke and they weren't going to eat boar meat on Christmas.

When Jacob returned to the stand Angie Swenson was standing underneath it and she was wearing shorts that were cut from old jeans and a t-shirt that said Garth Brooks on it and she had sneakers on and she was carrying a backpack and Jacob thought she looked beautiful.

Holy shit, he said.

Hi, she said.

Jacob said hi back and that he was sorry for swearing.

It's okay, Angie said.

Jacob came closer and when he did Angie tensed her grip on the straps of her pack and she looked over her shoulder like she did on the last day of school so Jacob stopped.

I'm glad you came, he said.

I can't stay.

Jacob nodded and said okay.

What're you doing out so early, Jacob said.

I go to Sentry every Thursday.

They don't open till eight.

I'm supposed to be there when it opens.

Jacob pointed to the stand.

You want to see it?

Angie looked back down the trail that led to the gravel road and then at the stand and nodded.

I can't stay though.

I know.

Okay.

Jacob pointed to the pack she was carrying and asked if she wanted him to carry it up for her and she seemed confused by this at first but then took it off and said okay. He put her pack on one shoulder and then picked up the gun and went up the ladder first and as he went up he gave her instructions on how to keep the ladder from swinging and twisting.

I'm not stupid, she said.

When he got to the top and was inside Jacob looked down at her through the floor.

That's good, Jacob said.

What's good?

It's good that you're not stupid.

Angie had no trouble climbing the ladder and the ladder didn't swing or twist as she did and when she got into the opening Jacob took her hand and helped her up and inside. She stood up and went to the wall and walked around the perimeter of the stand and looked into the woods and down the trail and through the woods into the field and when she was done she sat on the plywood box and pointed at the hatch.

Can you close that, she said.

Okay, Jacob said. You want me to bring up the ladder?

She nodded.

Okay.

Jacob pulled up the ladder and tucked it underneath the floor onto the branch that was supporting the stand and then he closed the hatch. Then he bundled up his sleeping bag and his pad and stuffed them into the corner and leaned back against the railing.

What do you think, Jacob said.

Angie was sitting with her ankles crossed and her hands tucked between her knees and the expression on her face crumpled a bit like she was going to cry but she didn't and then she took a deep breath and blew it out.

It's nice.

Thanks. I had to carry all the wood and my dad's tools up here and build it without electricity but I think it turned out okay.

How many did you get, Angie said.

What?

How many pigs did you get?

Oh. Two. I didn't scare you did I?

No.

I mean with the gunshots.

I know what you meant.

Okay, Jacob said. Did you know I'd be here?

Yes.

How?

Angie didn't say anything for a while and as they sat there in silence she took her hands from between her knees and set them on the box on either side of her.

I saw your light.

My light?

From the tower.

You mean last night?

Yes.

Where were you? On the beach?

Angie smiled a little bit and then shook her head and looked away into the woods.

On the bluff, she said.

Jacob thought about that and how he had unzipped his pants when he was on the tower to masturbate and he hoped she hadn't seen him. He thought it was too dark at the time for her to see him and besides if she had seen him like that she wouldn't have come here to see him now because she would have thought he was a deviant like her brother and father.

Could you see me? Jacob said.

I saw your light.

Jacob nodded.

Did they know you were there?

Angie shook her head and said no they didn't know she was there because they were too busy making out and taking their tops off to notice.

Jacob laughed and said, No I mean your—

He stopped talking because he hadn't spoken of her father and brother by name yet and he didn't know if it was okay. Then he thought that if he and Angie were going to be friends or maybe more than friends they would have to talk about them at some point.

I meant your dad and your brother, he said.

I know what you meant. I was messing with you.

Jacob smiled and thought about how smart and funny Angie was and how it was sad that she was scared and unhappy so much of the time and the more he thought about these things the more he wanted to kill her brother and her father.

They were passed out.

Drunk?

Yeah.

Angie looked at Jacob and she looked for a long time and she looked at every part of him including his eyes and his face and his hands and the holes in his jeans and his work boots. When she was done looking at him she looked at the floor and asked Jacob what the kids at school said about her.

I don't put stock in what people say.

But what do they say?

Jacob thought about this and about what he could say to her that wasn't a lie and wouldn't make her sad or hurt or angry or feel like he was giving her pity.

People don't say much, he said. Because they're scared of your brother.

Angie thought about this and then nodded as if to concede the point.

I have to go, she said.

When Angie said this Jacob's throat got tight and he felt like he was going to throw up and he was scared he wouldn't see her again for a long time and he didn't know what to say. Angie stood and then Jacob stood as well. She picked up her pack and unzipped the side pocket and took out a small cross made of copper and then zipped the pocket closed and held the cross out to Jacob.

My mother gave me this and it was a secret between her and me so they'll never know it's missing.

Jacob felt like he wanted to cry but he thought that he should be strong and so he swallowed and took the cross.

Don't you need it, he said.

I have hers, Angie said.

Okay. Thanks.

Jacob hung the cross on a nail in the tree that he sometimes used to hang his flashlight from when he wanted to read before he went to sleep and then he opened the hatch and set it on the floor and reached underneath and swept the ladder off the branch to uncoil it. Angie looked over the wall again and down the path and as she did Jacob hugged her and she tried to pull away but Jacob just held her tighter and after a while she stopped trying to pull away and she hugged him back and they stood there for some time neither of them moving or saying anything they just stood there holding each other and breathing.

When they let go of each other Angie had tears in her eyes and she wiped them away with her fingers and said thank you for showing me your stand. She stepped onto the ladder and when she did Jacob made to follow her.

Don't follow me, she said.

Okay, Jacob said.

* * *

Jacob was tending the register at the co-op because Bob Wilkins needed some time off to help with his son Trevor's wedding rehearsal in Edgewood and Jacob's father and Gary Schroeder were fixing a leaky burner on the grain dryer and that was a two man job. Jacob had changed the radio station and instead of country music playing over the co-op's intercom there was Nine Inch Nails playing which was the kind of music Gary Schroeder called scum rock but he was stuck under a grain dryer outside and there was no one to tell Jacob to turn it off.

In the morning a delivery had come in and since there were no customers Jacob was moving pallets of dog food and cat food from the dock into the store with the pallet jack and then hand stacking the bags on the shelves. As he worked he thought about Angie Swenson and how she had given him the cross that meant a lot to her and how he had hugged her. He wondered how long it had been since someone had hugged her and he thought he should get her something nice as well in case they saw each other again. The bell on top of the co-op door rang and Jacob put the bag of cat food he was holding onto the shelf and he took off his gloves and went to the front of the store.

What the fuck is this noise, Mark Swenson said. His words were garbled somewhat because he had a cigarette in his mouth when he said them. The door closed behind him and the bell rang again. He was holding a cultivator disc in his hand and he was caked in dried mud and the mud covered his boots and his coveralls up to his neck. His Fabco hat was tipped back and the brim was curled almost into a tube and he looked across the register at Jacob with his eyes drooping like he was drunk. Jacob went to the wall where the radio was and turned it off.

Thank the fuckin lord, Mark said. You in charge here now?

Yeah, Jacob said. You need something?

Do I need somethin? There's a fine fuckin way to meet a payin customer. You wanna try again?

As he said this Mark Swenson stepped into the store and took a long drag from his cigarette and then flicked it back against the door and it fell to the floor and sat there smoking on the mat. Jacob pointed to it and said you need to pick that up. Mark looked back at the cigarette on the floor and then at Jacob and then he walked around the counter to where Jacob was standing and Mark stood there pressing the edge of the disc against Jacob's chest breathing beer and cigarette breath into his face as he talked.

Tell you what, Mark said. You don't tell me what to fuckin do and what not to fuckin do. Hear me?

He pushed Jacob with the disc and Jacob stumbled backwards a little bit but then he regained his footing and he went back to where he was standing before.

You want it picked up? Mark said. Then pick it up your fuckin self.

Jacob was too angry to be scared and he looked into Mark's eyes and they were bloodshot and quivering either with rage or by the effect of some drug or other substance and Jacob said he wasn't going to pick up his cigarette and that he needed to pick it up himself and when Jacob said this Mark smiled a little bit.

You think you're hot shit don't you, Mark said. The old man puts you in charge and all of a sudden you're king shit. Ain't that right Jacob Miller? Yeah that's right I know you. You're the asshole thinks he's gonna fuck around with my sister.

When Mark said this about Angie Jacob didn't know how he found out and he wondered if Angie had told him about that day after school but then he thought about how scared she was that day and that she probably hadn't. Mark must have seen the surprise in Jacob's expression because he smiled a little bit and nodded his head and said that yes he knew about that day at the bike racks after school.

I got ways of finding shit out, he said. And you're extremely fuckin fortunate to be still breathing Jacob Miller.

Fuck you, Jacob said.

Mark laughed at this and said that he understood why

Jacob was so upset and that it was because he was sexually frustrated as a result of being rejected by his sister Angie and that maybe he wasn't the ladies man he thought he was. After he said this Mark leaned in and placed his head so that he was speaking directly into Jacob's ear.

She needs a real man, Mark said.

The bell on the door of the co-op rang and as it did Jacob put his hands on Mark's chest and pushed him away and Mark fell backwards onto the counter. The cultivator disc came out of his hand and it clattered across the floor to where Jacob's father and Gary Schroeder were entering the store.

You son of a bitch I know what you do to her, Jacob said. You can't treat her like that you son of a bitch!

Jacob ran to where Mark had fallen against the counter but was now back on his feet and Jacob tried to tackle him to the floor but Mark braced himself and he stood fast and pushed Jacob away and as he did he struck Jacob with a backhand across his face. Jacob stumbled backwards and his father was behind Jacob now and he caught him and held him against his struggle to free himself and launch another attack on Mark Swenson. Gary Schroeder put himself between Jacob and Mark and was extending his arms to hold them away from each other and Jacob was struggling against the hold his father had on him and he was screaming and cursing at Mark and Mark was repositioning his Fabco hat on his head.

You don't know shit, Mark said. You'd better watch yourself.

Jacob's father turned Jacob around and took him to the office at the front of the store and Jacob was still struggling but it was less spirited now. Jacob's father called over his shoulder to ask Gary to assist Mark with the repair of his cultivator disc and to tell them both that there would be no charge for the service. When they got inside the office Jacob's father closed the door and put Jacob in the chair by the door and Jacob was shaking and there was spittle hanging from his chin.

Christ Jacob what the hell are you thinking, Jacob's father said. You trying to get yourself killed?

Jacob wiped the spittle from his chin by dragging the sleeve of his shirt across it.

It's a damn good thing Gary saw his truck pull up. I had a feeling something like this would happen.

Jacob didn't say anything.

Christ, Jacob's father said. I never should've told you that about the Swenson girl.

I would've found out anyway, Jacob said.

Jacob's father said that even though standing up for people who can't stand up for themselves seems like the right thing to do sometimes you just can't.

Because it's complicated, Jacob said.

Don't sass me Jacob.

Jacob didn't say anything.

The Swensons bring us a lot of business, Jacob's father said. And if they decide to take it elsewhere I don't know if we'd make it.

Jacob rubbed the spot on his face where Mark had struck him with a backhand fist. He thought about the time his father and mother had been fighting because his mother had written a check at Sentry that had bounced because business at the co-op had been slow that month and Jacob's father had to pay Gary Schroeder and Bob Wilkins before he could pay himself because a man looks out for his neighbors before himself.

It's not right, Jacob said. People can't do whatever they want just because they've got money.

Jacob's father shook his head and looked away from Jacob and out the window of the office and into the store. He watched Mark Swenson open the door to the co-op and go outside and he watched as the door closed behind Mark and as the bell attached to the wall above the door rang.

Sometimes they can Jacob, he said. I don't want any more problems with the Swensons. Understand?

It isn't right, Jacob said.

Do you understand Jacob?

I understand.

Good.

It isn't right, dad.

I know it isn't.

* * *

Jacob pulled the door to Mr. Foster's barn open on its slide until there was enough space for Mr. Foster's four wheeler to go through and then Jacob got in the seat and drove the four wheeler out of the barn and then got off to close the door behind him. He kicked the wheels of the trailer he had attached to the four wheeler and double checked the hitch to make sure it was pinned and then got back in the seat and drove out of the barnyard and onto the field road that ran next to Mr. Foster's soybeans. He could see Indian Bluff in the distance as he drove and he wondered if Angie was up there now and he wondered how often she went there and whether or not she was thinking of him right then as he was thinking of her. He decided he would ask her these and all manner of other questions when he saw her again.

At the edge of the woods the field road narrowed and the surface was uneven and pocked with holes that would cause the trailer to jump and rattle as Jacob drove so he slowed his speed to guard against damaging it. He was still thinking about Angie but now he was wishing she was on the back of the four wheeler with her hands around his waist to keep her balance as they navigated the uneven surface of the road.

Jacob stopped the four wheeler when he got to the dead boar that was nearest the stand and he got off and put on his work gloves and took hold of the boar two legs to a hand. It was too heavy for Jacob to lift into the trailer so he stood there for some time thinking about how he was going to get it inside. He dragged the boar to the back of the trailer and lowered the tailgate and then he unlatched the dump box and raised it. From the toolbox on the back of the four wheeler he took a length of rope and he tied one end of the rope around the boar's neck and the other end he looped over the crossbar at the front end of the trailer. Jacob sat on the ground next to the dead boar and it smelled of earth and rot and excrement and he pulled on the rope and pushed the boar up the incline of the tailgate with his feet until it was on the bed of the trailer. He got up and unlatched the dump box all the while keeping tension on the rope to keep the boar from sliding off the trailer and then he let the dump box down and latched it. Jacob untied the rope from the boar's neck and then pushed the boar fully onto the bed of the trailer and closed the tailgate. He wondered what Angie would think if she had been watching him and he wondered if she would be impressed with his ability to load a dead boar into a trailer by himself and he wondered if she would say how smart and clever he was or if she would just think it was disgusting.

Jacob thought about how he could get the second boar into the trailer with the first one already in there and he wondered whether or not he could raise and lower the dump box with the extra weight all the while keeping tension on the rope tied to the second boar. In the end he decided to unload the first boar and come back for the second one which would take more time but Jacob decided it couldn't be helped.

He started the four wheeler and drove on the field road and now the trailer didn't bounce and rattle as much because of the extra weight inside and then he came to the place where the field narrowed to a point and there was no more cropland just woods. The field road continued into the woods as an off road trail and Jacob followed it to the clearing where Mr. Foster had dug a large pit with his skidsteer and put barbed wire around it. Inside the pit were the bodies of pigs from Mr. Foster's swine house that had been infected with a virus and had either died or were unusable for food and likely to infect the rest of the house and were put down. They were covered with a layer of dirt from the pile of it Mr. Foster had made when excavating the pit to keep the flies and the odor down. On the near side of the pit there was a gate fashioned into the barbed wire and Jacob unfastened the post and doubled the barbed wire back over itself to create an opening and then he put the post on the ground.

Jacob backed the trailer to the edge of the pit and lowered the tailgate and unlatched the dump box and tried to raise it but he had to stand on the back of the four wheeler to gain the leverage to lift the box with the extra weight of the boar inside and when he did this the dead boar slid off the trailer and into the pit. He drove back to the place where the second boar had fallen and he thought that maybe instead of putting it in the trailer he would just tie the rope around its neck and drag it to the pit but then he decided not to. He thought that dragging the boar might damage more of Mr. Foster's beans or that it might cause the boar's head to come off which would make a bigger mess than he started with so he lowered the tailgate and raised the dump box and tied the rope to the second boar's neck. Jacob stood there looking at the second boar and its tusks were bigger and longer and more curved than those of the first one and he decided he wanted to use them to make necklaces for himself and for Angie.

    Jacob went to the stand and lowered the ladder with the length of quarter round and climbed up and raised the hatch and opened the plywood box and found the backsaw he kept there among other tools for maintenance of the stand. He closed the box and dropped the backsaw to the ground through the opening in the floor and climbed down and picked up the saw and went back to where the four wheeler and the trailer and the boar with a rope around its neck were. The backsaw was designed to cut wood and it hadn't been sharpened in some time because Jacob didn't have a file to sharpen it with in the stand so it took a long time to saw the tusks from the boar's head and when he was done Jacob was sweating and his arm was sore from the effort. He put the saw and the tusks on the seat of the four wheeler and rested for a time before repeating the procedure he had used on the first boar to load the second one into the trailer. It took Jacob less time to load the second boar into the trailer even though it was bigger than the first because he had learned the process on the first one and he didn't need to use trial and error to figure things out. Jacob thought that this logic would apply to many different things and he decided that when he made the necklaces he would make his own first and then he would make Angie's after that because he wanted hers to be of the highest quality possible.

After Jacob had dumped the second boar into the pit he took the shovel from its stays in the trailer bed and shoveled dirt onto the bodies of the boars he had shot until they were covered and then he closed the barbed wire gate and drove back to the stand. Mr. Foster had told Jacob that he didn't have to return the four wheeler and trailer right away in case the boar that got away came back and Jacob shot it and needed to take it to the pit as well. Jacob didn't want to spook the boar by parking in the field so he parked the four wheeler and trailer in the woods under the stand.

When Jacob climbed back into the stand he was tired and thirsty and hungry but he didn't care because he wanted to make the necklaces out of the second boar's tusks more than he wanted to eat or drink. He put the backsaw into the plywood box and took out the hand drill and the bits for it which were wrapped together with a rubber band and he selected one that looked sharp enough to drill through boar tusk and he chucked it in the drill. Jacob held one of the tusks on the floor with his knee and with the hand drill he made a hole in one end near the place where he had separated it from the boar. From the plywood box he took the can of spray lubricant and the steel wool and cloth that he used to keep his father's tools from becoming corroded and he used these things to clean the tusk until it was no longer fouled with dirt and blood and it reflected the light when he turned it in his hand. Jacob prepared the second tusk in the same way and then he took the cross Angie had given him from the nail on the tree and he unhooked the clasp and put the chain through the hole in the tusk he had chosen as his own and hooked the clasp and put everything back on the nail. He looked at it and thought it looked pretty good.

In the box was a length of twine that Jacob had used to secure his sleeping bag in a roll when he first brought it to the stand and he took the twine from the box and put it through the hole in Angie's tusk and cut it to length with his pocketknife and tied the ends together. He put Angie's necklace on the nail next to his own and looked at both of them and decided that he would carve their names into them when he got the chance.

The sun was below the trees on the other side of Mr. Foster's field and it was getting dark and Jacob hadn't eaten supper yet because he didn't know how long it would take to put the dead boars in the pit so he had told his mother and father that he would eat at the stand. He took the Coleman stove and cookpot that he used in these kinds of situations out of the plywood box and he filled the pot with water from a jug of it he had brought in his pack and he lit the stove and put the pot on the burner. There was a box of cheesy noodles in his pack as well which he had found in the kitchen cupboard and Jacob opened it and dumped its contents into the water and stirred it with a spoon and then he sat. In the woods he heard a whippoorwill call and he tried to remember what his father had told him about their song and how it related to the weather but he couldn't so he just listened to it and when it stopped singing Jacob stirred the cheesy noodles again. When he was done stirring he put the spoon down on the floor and when he did this he heard footsteps on the ground outside the stand. Jacob stood and went to the wall and looked down at the trail and he could see someone there and they weren't moving now they were just standing but he couldn't see who it was because they were a silhouette in the dark.

Who's there, Jacob said.

It's Angie.

Jacob put out his hand to motion for her to stay even though she probably couldn't see it and when he did this he could feel that his hand was shaking a little.

Stay there, Jacob said. I'll give you some light.

He turned around and searched blindly in the box for his flashlight because it was almost full dark now and the blue light from the burner of his stove didn't reach over the side of the box. Jacob's hands were still shaking and he was nervous which was unusual Jacob thought because people didn't make him nervous even girls. When he found the flashlight Jacob took it to the wall and turned it on and lit the ground where Angie had been standing but she wasn't there anymore.

I'm down here, she said.

Jacob lifted the hatch and pointed the flashlight through the floor and Angie was underneath the stand and she had on a backpack and she was holding onto the ladder and she had one foot on the ground and her other foot was on the ladder. Her bike was leaning against the tree and light reflected off the metal baskets that were attached to the back of it for use in hauling groceries.

Can I come up, she said.

Yes of course you can.

Angie climbed into the stand and Jacob raised the ladder and put it on the branch and closed the hatch.

Did I surprise you, she said.

A little.

Jacob took her pack and put it in the corner of the stand and with the flashlight he illuminated the sleeping pad that was on the floor next to the tree and then they sat next to each other on the pad and Jacob turned off the flashlight and they talked in the dark.

I'm glad you came, Jacob said.

Me too.

How long can you stay?

All night.

When Jacob heard this he was even more excited than he had been before but now his hands weren't shaking and he didn't feel nervous anymore.

Are you serious?

I'm serious.

What about Mark and your dad?

What about them.

They out drinking or something?

No they're done drinking.

Passed out?

Yeah.

Already?

Yeah.

All night you think?

Angie thought about this for a while as if deciding whether or not to tell him something and then she must have decided that she would because she told Jacob that the last time she was at Sentry she bought some sleeping pills and that when she got home she ground them up into a powder and put the powder in a plastic bag in her room. Then she told him how she had put some of the powder into the beers she brought them earlier that evening.

    Wow, Jacob said. You're kind of a badass aren't you?

    Kind of.

    What happened when they drank it?

    I don't want to talk about them anymore okay?

    Okay.

    They were both watching the blue flame from the Coleman stove flicker under the cookpot and now and then a little bit of yellow flame would try to climb out from underneath the pot and scale the side of it but then it would die out.

    Did you eat supper yet, Jacob said.

    No.

    Well we can eat together then. Like on a date.

    When Jacob said this he thought that maybe he shouldn't have because it might make Angie feel sad or uncomfortable because she couldn't go on dates like other people but he didn't really have to worry about it because as he was thinking this Angie had started to laugh.

    What, Jacob said.

    Do you bring all of your dates here, she said.

    Jacob thought about this and said that come to think of it she was the first girl that had ever been in the stand and that not even his own mother had been in it.

    Well aren't I special, Angie said.

    Yes you are, Jacob said.

* * *

When Jacob woke it was early and there was only a little

bit of light in the canopy above the stand and there were birds of all kinds calling in the woods and he could see his breath in the air because the weather was cool. He was next to Angie on the floor and he had given her the sleeping pad to sleep on and he had unzipped his sleeping bag so that it was flat like a blanket and they had slept under that together.

Jacob rose and pulled the sleeping bag up so that it would cover her more completely and offer more warmth and when he did he saw the necklace he had given to her the night before. It was around her neck on the twine and it sat on the floor of the stand next to her head and Jacob looked at Angie's hair and it was tangled and covered her eyes a little bit and it was matted on her neck and he thought about how beautiful she looked and he wondered how anyone could be cruel to her. The more he thought about this the more he thought he would never be able to understand it and the only way that it would make even a little bit of sense would be if there was a special place in hell waiting for Dale and Mark Swenson.

Jacob stood and put on his boots and tied them and then he put on his jacket and as he was doing this Angie stirred and said what time is it.

It's early. You can sleep.

Where are you going?

To see if I can get that other boar.

Okay.

I'll be close by. Just at the edge of the field.

How am I supposed to sleep if you shoot a boar?

I might not.

But you might.

Yes. I might.

Then I might be able to sleep and I might not.

Right.

Okay.

Jacob opened the plywood box and took out the shotgun and two shells and the gun he put over his shoulder and the shells he put in his pocket. He closed the box and opened the hatch and pushed the ladder from the branch and stepped down onto it and when he looked at Angie to say goodbye he could hear the sound of her breathing and it was heavy and regular and he knew that she had fallen back to sleep.

Jacob closed the hatch behind him and climbed down the ladder and as he did he thought that Angie probably didn't sleep very well as a rule because of her father and brother being in the same house and because she would always be worried about what they were doing or what they were thinking about doing. He thought that by comparison she probably wasn't worried about whether he would or wouldn't shoot at a boar.

In the woods at the edge of the field was a blind that Jacob had built the day before and it was built with sticks and vines and leaves and it was in the shape of a teepee and on one side was an opening that he could use for going in and out of it and Jacob stepped inside and took the shells out of his pocket and sat. He loaded the shells into the gun and cycled the first one and then he looked out into the field through a gap in the blind and he could see some deer that were eating Mr. Foster's beans and there was one that was watching the blind because it had probably seen him go into it and was keeping watch for the others and its breath was visible in the cool air.

After a while the deer that was on lookout started eating beans again and when it did Jacob heard something behind him and when he turned and looked through a gap in that side of the blind he could see another deer walking up the path from the gravel road. It stopped under the stand and it looked at the four wheeler and trailer that were parked there and it didn't move but just stood there breathing steam. After looking at the four wheeler and the trailer for a while the deer became spooked and it twitched where it stood and then it ran past Jacob in his blind to the field and it was snorting and blowing and when it reached the place in the field where the other deer were they all started to run and snort and blow steam. When the deer were in the middle of the field they stopped running and they all stood and looked back at the place where Jacob sat in his blind and the deer that had come from the woods was still snorting and Jacob knew it was the same deer because he had watched it run through the field.

Soon all of the deer were eating soybeans again and then Jacob looked past the deer that had come from the woods behind him and on the other side of the field was a boar and it was looking across the field and it seemed to be looking at Jacob in his blind but he couldn't be sure. He didn't know if it was the same boar that had gotten away when he shot the other two but to Jacob one boar was the same as another. Jacob pushed the muzzle of the gun through the blind as quietly as he could and when he did the boar didn't move nor did it give any clues that it saw him or was startled and Jacob thought that this was a good sign.

After a time the boar appeared to grow uneasy and it turned and went into the woods and disappeared from view and when it turned Jacob could see that one of its tusks was shorter than the other because it was broken. At the same time the boar went into the woods the deer in the field looked up from their eating and began to blow and snort. Jacob heard something behind him moving by the stand and when he turned around he saw Mark Swenson standing by the four wheeler and he was smoking and looking up at the stand and he was wearing his Fabco hat and he had on a flannel shirt and jeans that were fouled with dirt and manure. He was talking but he was doing it in a low voice and Jacob couldn't make out what he was saying but by the tone of it he thought that Mark was angry. Jacob sat there just watching and he thought that Mark didn't know he was in the blind only twenty paces away and even though this seemed like a good thing Jacob's hands began to shake and he was feeling nervous again because he had the feeling that something terrible was about to happen.

Mark looked down from the stand and when he did he went around the tree to where Angie's bike was and he stumbled as he approached it and he fell to his knees on the ground and looked at it. Now Jacob could hear what Mark was saying but because Mark still had the cigarette in the corner of his mouth and he was probably drunk or under the influence of drugs the words were somewhat garbled.

You fuckin whore, Mark said. What did you do?

Mark's body was shaking and his voice was trembling when he said this and Angie must have heard him talking because Jacob heard her stirring in the stand and then he saw her head appear over the top of the wall and by the look on her face Jacob could tell that she was terrified.

Jacob where are you, she said. Jacob!

When Mark heard Angie say this he stood up and took a handgun out of the back of his jeans and Jacob hadn't seen it there because it had been covered by his flannel shirt and then Mark raised the gun and shot into the bottom of the stand. Angie screamed and fell to the floor and she was crying and yelling for Jacob.

You fuckin whore, Mark said.

Mark moved the aim of his gun to follow the sound of Angie's voice and the sound of her movements in the stand and as he did this Jacob stepped out through the opening in the blind and raised the shotgun. When Mark saw him emerge from the blind he lowered his gun to aim it at Jacob but as he did Jacob shot Mark Swenson in the neck and the blast made Angie scream again. Mark fell back against the tree and arterial blood was pumping out of his neck and then he fell to the ground on his side and he was trying to talk but there was blood coming from his mouth and his voice was labored and wet and then he stopped tying to talk and then he didn't move anymore. Jacob stood there looking at Mark on the ground under the stand and then he looked into the woods and down the path and into Mr. Foster's field to see if anyone had seen what happened but there was no one and the deer were gone from the field as well. He looked up at the stand.

Angie, he said. Are you hurt?

Angie stood and looked over the wall and down at Jacob and she wasn't crying anymore but Jacob thought that she still looked terrified.

I'm okay, she said. What's happening?

Jacob stood there looking at Mark who was on the ground under the stand not moving and he thought about what he had just done and he thought that when he was doing it he hadn't thought about it first he just did it because he was numb and scared and trying to keep Mark from shooting Angie through the floor of the stand. Then he thought about how the co-op would probably have to close now because the Swensons wouldn't be spending their money there anymore and how his mother would have to be careful when she wrote checks at Sentry and how his father would have to tell Gary Schroeder and Bob Wilkins that they would need to look for jobs elsewhere and he wondered if Mr. Wilkins would be able to afford the expenses of his son's wedding and Jacob thought all of these things as he looked at Mark Swenson not moving under the stand but these things really didn't matter that much because all that mattered was that Mark wouldn't be able to hurt Angie anymore.

Nothing, Jacob said. It's okay.

Jacob went to where Mark was lying on the ground and he was still aiming the shotgun at him because he wasn't sure that he was dead but when he saw the condition of Mark's neck and the amount of blood that had come out of his mouth he knew that he was in fact dead. The cigarette that Mark had been smoking when he was still alive was on the ground and it was still smoking and Jacob crushed it with his boot and then he took the gun from Mark's hand.

Is he dead, Angie said.

Jacob looked up and Angie was looking down through the floor of the stand and she was holding the hatch open and Jacob nodded and said that yes he was dead.

Angie came down the ladder and stood next to Jacob and looked down at her dead brother and her face crumpled a little like she was going to cry but she didn't and then she wiped the tears from her face that she had cried before.

Good, she said.

Jacob looked at Angie but he didn't say anything and then

he took her in his arms even though he had a gun in each hand and they stood there for some time both of them not saying anything. Jacob let her go and they went to where the four wheeler and the trailer were to put some distance between them and Mark's dead body and then Jacob put the guns in the trailer.

What should we do, Angie said.

Jacob thought about this and decided that he wasn't afraid of what the sheriff would do or what his father or anyone in town would do or think or say about the situation because they all knew what kind of person Mark Swenson was and if he and Angie told the truth about what happened they would all believe it. What Jacob was afraid of was what Dale Swenson would do when he found out that Jacob had shot his son Mark and also of what he would do when he found out that Jacob was friends or maybe more than friends with his daughter Angie. He thought that Dale would probably kill him or Angie or both of them or that he would be even more cruel to Angie than he was already.

I don't know, Jacob said. What do you think we should do?

I don't know.

Jacob thought that Angie did know but didn't want to say because she didn't want to pressure him into making a decision either way so Jacob thought about it a little longer.

I think if your dad finds out we're in trouble, Jacob said.

I think so too.

He might kill us.

I think he would.

He can't find out.

No.

I don't think Mark knew you were here when he came,

Jacob said.

Okay.

So I don't think your dad knows either.

Probably not.

Jacob thought some more and decided that if Mark just disappeared and never came back they might be okay and then he decided to put Mark into the pit with Mr. Foster's dead pigs and with the boars that Jacob had shot. He thought he would have to put Mark deep under the pigs that were already in the pit to keep him hidden in case scavengers or the weather exposed the dirt covering the pit's contents. He knew it would be a terrible job and that he would probably become sick and vomit while he was doing it but he couldn't think of anything else to do. Jacob told Angie about his plan and she said okay.

While I'm doing that you go to Sentry, Jacob said.

I want to help you at the pit.

I don't think that's a good idea.

Angie said that she felt guilty for getting Jacob involved with her and her brother and her father and that as long as they were in this situation together she thought they should do the dirty jobs in equal shares. Jacob told her not to feel guilty about anything because he wanted to get himself involved with her and that there would be plenty of dirty jobs to go around in their current situation and that it was important to do everything like normal until someone noticed that Mark was missing.

Angie thought about this for a while and said okay.

You can help me put him in the trailer but then you should go, Jacob said.

Okay.

Jacob took the guns out of the trailer and he put Mark's

handgun on the seat of the four wheeler and then he took the shotgun up into the stand and unloaded the shell that was still in it and put it in the box with the rest of them and he put the gun and the box of shells back in the plywood box and took out the plastic tarp. He picked up Angie's backpack and put it on his shoulder and went to the wall and looked into the woods and down the trail and into the field but he didn't see anyone.

When Jacob came down from the stand Angie was standing at the bottom of the ladder looking at her brother. Jacob didn't know if he should say something to her or if he should stand next to her or what he should do and in the end he didn't do anything except tend to his business. He put Angie's backpack on the ground by her bike and then he spread the tarp over the bed of the trailer and when he was done with these things Angie was still standing by her brother looking at him and not saying anything or moving. Jacob went to her side and told her that he was ready to put Mark in the trailer.

I'm not happy or sad, Angie said.

What?

I feel like I should be either happy or sad but I'm neither.

You should be whatever you are, Jacob said.

I guess I'm neither then.

That sounds about right.

Angie said that she agreed on the point since there wasn't a way to make herself feel otherwise.

Are you ready, Jacob said.

Angie didn't say anything for a while and then she started to breathe faster and when Jacob looked at her she looked like she was going to cry again but she didn't.

He was so mean to me, she said.

Jacob took her hand and held it but he didn't say anything.

I can't ever have babies, Jacob.

Jacob looked at her and said he was sorry and then Angie shook her head and said that it didn't matter because she didn't think she'd ever want to have babies anyway. Jacob thought about this and realized that he never gave much thought to having babies or to not having babies himself but then he thought that if you were in a situation like Angie was you probably did think about babies sometimes and about what kind of world you would want to bring them into.

He would've done it, Angie said.

Done what?

Killed us both.

I think he would've.

Then he would've killed himself.

Probably.

Like that kid up in Darlington.

Yeah.

It's much better this way.

Yes it is.

You did the right thing, Angie said.

I know.

When they were done talking they picked up Mark's body each of them to an end and put him on the tarp in the trailer and then they folded the tarp over to cover him and they weighted the loose edges of it with stones they found on the ground. Jacob picked up branches and vines and leaves from the ground as well and was putting these on the tarp to camouflage it but then he thought this might look more suspicious than the tarp by itself so he took them off. He looked at the shape of the tarp with Mark Swenson's body under it and decided that it could pass for two boars under a tarp if you didn't look too long at it. While Jacob was putting plant matter on the tarp and taking it off and looking at the shape of the tarp Angie put her backpack in one of the baskets on her bike and rolled the bike to where Jacob was and she leaned her bike onto the ground and took Jacob in her arms and hugged him and Jacob hugged her back. She said thank you for saving my life to which Jacob said you're welcome. He said that he was glad things worked out like they did and then Angie looked at him and they were still in each other's arms and then she kissed him. They kissed for a while and then Angie looked at Jacob again and he looked back at her.

My hero, Angie said.

Jacob smiled a little at this.

Anyone would've done it, he said.

But anyone didn't.

Okay.

They let each other go and Angie picked up her bike and Jacob took the handgun off the seat of the four wheeler and sat.

Do you know where they keep this, he said.

Yeah I'll put it back.

Okay. Be careful.

Angie said she would and then Jacob gave her the gun and she put it in her backpack and zipped it closed.

Be careful yourself, she said.

Jacob said he would and he started the four wheeler and drove it around in an arc so that the four wheeler was pointed in the right direction and then he stopped with the engine still running.

Come back when you can, he said.

I will.

Good luck.

You too.

Jacob drove onto the field road and when he did he could feel the four wheeler shake like it had gone over an obstruction but he knew that it hadn't so he looked back and he saw that Angie's bike was on its side in the woods by his boar blind and Angie was walking next to the trailer and she was beating her dead brother Mark's head with a piece of wood. The wood was thick and heavy like the stump of a small tree and it took some effort for her to lift it and when she let it down the shape of Mark's head distorted and shifted under the tarp. Jacob stopped the four wheeler and watched Angie hit her brother's head with the wood some more and she was crying now and she was screaming at Mark as she hit him but Jacob couldn't hear what she was saying over the sound of the four wheeler's engine. He didn't turn off the four wheeler because he figured what Angie was saying was between her and her brother.

When she was done Angie dropped the piece of wood and walked back to her bike and she was still crying and she staggered a little as she walked and she didn't say anything to Jacob nor did she look back at him. Jacob sat on the four wheeler with its engine running and watched as she picked her bike up from the ground and walked it down the trail that went to the gravel road.

* * *

It was late in the morning when Jacob returned to the

stand and the day had warmed greatly since the deer had been feeding on soybeans and blowing steam in the air and Jacob thought about how the events of the early morning seemed much farther in the past than they actually were. He had buried Mark Swenson under the pigs in Mr. Foster's pit and his boots and his clothes and his gloves were soaked with filth and stank of mud and rot but the job was done and no one had seen him do it. Jacob parked the four wheeler and the trailer under the stand and turned off the engine and sat there for some time thinking about what he had yet to do.

There was a considerable amount of blood on the ground where Mark had died and he would have to do something about that. He didn't know if his father would notice the bullet hole Mark had made in the floor of the stand or question him about it but he thought that maybe he would do something about that as well. His boots and his clothes and the tarp and the bed of the trailer and the seat of Mr. Foster's four wheeler were fouled with the smell of death and would have to be washed or burned and he would need to bathe himself in the lake before he went home. As he thought about these things it didn't really bother Jacob that he had to do them because he was doing them for Angie and also because she had endured far worse things than cleaning up blood and washing away the smell of rot.

Jacob got off the four wheeler and took off his shirt and put it on the tarp that was folded and weighted with stones in the trailer and he went to the edge of Mr. Foster's field because there was a breeze there. He stood on the field road and the breeze cooled him and the sun dried the sweat from his body and when he looked across the field he saw that there was a boar watching him from under a tree. It was the same boar that he had seen in the early morning and he knew it was the same boar because of its broken tusk.

Jacob didn't think about trying to get the shotgun to shoot the boar because when he looked at it he realized that the boar with the broken tusk was the reason he had been in the blind and not in the stand when Mark Swenson had arrived and started shooting. Jacob didn't know for sure what would have happened if he had been in the stand and he didn't know if he or Angie or both of them would have been shot and killed but he did know that things turned out all right the way they did happen. Jacob looked at the boar for a while and the boar looked back and when Jacob was done looking at the boar he turned and went to the blind he had built and kicked it down and when he looked back across the field the boar was gone.

He went back to where the four wheeler and the trailer were parked under the stand and he thought about the boar with the broken tusk and as he thought about that boar in particular he thought about boars in general and how they fit into the circle of things.

PART 2

The Hero's Reprise

Three Years Later

JACOB sat in the sand of Indian Lake beach and drank from a can of soda that had a little bit of vodka added to it from the flask of it they had brought with them in Angie's bag. He watched Angie swim in the lake and she was shivering because the water was cold too cold for Jacob to swim but it wasn't for Angie because she wanted to catch up with all of the swimming she had missed out on when she was younger. They were alone on the beach but there was a boat on the lake and in the boat was Jacob's father and he was fishing the far shore because it was fall and Jacob's father always said that the fall was the best time to take pike from the lake. Jacob knew that it really didn't matter what time of year it was because you could catch pike at any time it was just that his father liked to fish in the fall because the lake wasn't so crowded and it wasn't so hot.

Come swim with me Jacob, Angie said. She was lying on her stomach in the shallow water with just her head above the surface and her teeth were chattering.

I didn't bring my suit, Jacob said.

Angie looked behind her at Jacob's father on the other side of the lake. She looked at Jacob again and spoke in a low voice because Jacob had told her how far sound can travel over water.

Just go naked. There's no one here except your dad.

Jacob laughed at this and then he began to speak in a low voice as well.

You'd like that wouldn't you, he said.

Angie smiled and made a clucking sound and called him a chicken and asked him what he was worried about.

The water's too cold.

Don't be such a baby. I'm in it.

That's not what I'm worried about.

Then what are you worried about?

I don't want you to see my dick and balls all shriveled up and small.

What?

From the cold water.

That's what happens?

Yeah.

Angie thought about this a little and then she stood up and she was smiling and water ran down her body and Jacob looked at her in her bathing suit and it was a one piece but he still thought it was sexy.

I have to see that, she said.

After she said this Angie ran up to where Jacob was sitting and she was dripping cold water on him and laughing and she grabbed Jacob's arm and tried to pull him to his feet and when this didn't work she started pulling at the legs of his pants trying to pull them down. Jacob was bigger and stronger than she was so none of this worked and she couldn't pull him down to the water or pull his pants down and instead Jacob pulled her into the sand on her back and he sat on her. She pushed against him and struggled and she was laughing and coughing with the effort and Jacob just sat there straddled on her stomach until she became tired and stopped. When she got her breath back she spoke in a low voice again and she was still laughing a little from the weight of Jacob's body pressing down on her.

What're you worried about, she said. I know how big it really is.

Angie smiled at Jacob and her eyebrows were raised in a mischievous expression and then Jacob bent down and kissed her. She kissed him back and put her hands on his chest and when they were done kissing she pushed him over onto his side and she turned to lay next to him and she was covered with sand that had stuck to the water on her body and Jacob looked at the sand that was on her neck and face and in her hair and he thought she looked beautiful.

Are you going to miss me, Jacob said.

I always miss you. But you always come back.

Always.

Maybe I can come and stay with you next weekend.

Jacob thought about this and remembered that his roommate wouldn't be able to go home from school the following weekend either because he was taking the same exam as Jacob on Saturday but Jacob thought that his roommate would understand and would stay with someone else so that Jacob and Angie could have the room to themselves.

You won't run off with some college guy will you, Jacob said.

Angie laughed and said no because she already had one.

Then I would love for you to come, Jacob said.

Really?

Really.

Is it okay for girls to stay there?

Guys have their girlfriends over all the time.

For the whole weekend?

Yeah.

Angie made a squealing noise because she was very excited and she kissed Jacob and said that she couldn't wait.

Me too, Jacob said.

Angie rolled onto her back and closed her eyes and she was still smiling and Jacob watched her as she lay there drying in the sun.

You need to get out of here, Jacob said.

I will.

I mean out of this town.

I know what you meant.

It's not fair you couldn't graduate, Jacob said.

We already talked about this.

I know but it wasn't your fault.

Angie turned her head on the sand and looked at Jacob and told him that life isn't fair sometimes but that she would have enough credits by the end of the semester and that when she did Mr. and Mrs. Tanner said they would pay part of her tuition for college since that's what they signed up for when they took her in.

And besides Mr. O'Malley gave me a raise, Angie said. I can save up for a car and then we can see each other whenever we want.

Jacob said that he understood the situation and that he understood her plan but that wasn't why he wanted her to leave. He said that the reason he wanted her to leave was because he didn't like that she was living in the same town as her father and that he would feel better if she was someplace else since he wasn't around as much to look after her like he could before.

We don't need to worry about him, Angie said.

Of course we do.

No we don't. He can't hurt anyone. He's weak. Besides he never leaves his house.

I saw his truck on the bluff road last weekend, Jacob said.

Angie sat up and brushed the dried sand from her skin and from her bathing suit with her hand and said that her father only goes up to the bluff to mourn the loss of his son Mark and to wait there for him to come back and to call out to him.

Besides it's only half a mile from his house, she said. And that's as far as he ever goes.

She turned onto her stomach and took a can of soda from the bag she had brought and opened it and poured some of its contents in the sand and looked over her shoulder at Jacob's father in the boat and then she took the flask of vodka from her bag and poured some of it into her can and then put the flask back into her bag.

How do you know he's weak, Jacob said.

Because he doesn't do anything. He doesn't work the land. He only eats what he grows in that stupid garden. I'd be surprised if he could even shoot a deer now. Let alone dress it out.

Well I'll feel better when you get out of here.

Fine but don't worry okay?

Okay.

They sat on the beach and drank spiked soda from a can and talked and watched the boat drift against the opposite shore of the lake. After a while they could hear Jacob's father stow his fishing gear and he made a racket of sound against the bottom of the boat as he did and the din traveled over and through the water and echoed from the bluff behind them in a concord of sound as if to announce the coming of some royal presence to the shores of the lake. They knew that Jacob's father would be coming soon to pick them up in the boat so they poured the contents of their soda cans into the lake and washed the insides with lake water and put the empty cans into Angie's bag. From the package of mint flavored gum that was in the bag they each took a piece and chewed it to mask the scent of alcohol on their breath. Angie used a towel to brush away the sand that remained stuck on her skin and on her bathing suit and when she was done she put the towel in her bag and then she put on her shorts over her bathing suit and they sat.

What do you want to do tonight, Angie said.

I could come over for a movie, Jacob said.

What do you want to watch?

It doesn't matter.

Okay.

* * *

Jacob's father took Angie to the Tanners' house which was where she had lived ever since Dale Swenson had lost custody of her as a result of beating her and putting her in the hospital because he thought she was hiding something about the disappearance of his son Mark. Mr. and Mrs. Tanner were visiting their daughter Megan and their son Kyle at their college overnight so there was no one else there when Jacob and his father left her which made Jacob nervous but Angie told him not to be because she could take care of herself and besides he would be back soon anyway. Jacob's father said he agreed with Angie's side on the matter and that he wouldn't keep Jacob long just long enough to have his help in storing the boat and fishing gear.

Jacob and his father went home and they unhitched the boat and cleaned the fishing gear out of it and covered it with canvas and stored the battery and the motor and when they were done Jacob took a shower to wash the sand from his body and when he was ready to leave his father told Jacob that he was proud of him.

For what, Jacob said.

For being a good friend to Angie.

She needed one.

Yes she did.

She makes me happy too.

I know. And I'm ashamed of how I looked at things regarding Dale and Mark.

Everyone else looked at it the same.

You didn't.

Jacob didn't say anything to this because he didn't know what to say.

I'm sorry for that, Jacob's father said.

Okay.

I don't know what happened to Mark Swenson, Jacob's father said. I don't know if anyone will ever know what happened to him. You know I'm not a church going man but I think that maybe whatever happened to him was because of fate or divine intervention or some such thing. To put you and her together.

I don't know about that, Jacob said.

Jacob's father smiled a little and shook his head and told Jacob that he didn't know about that either and he told Jacob not to listen to him because he was just a rambling old man and then he gave Jacob the keys to his mother's car. He told Jacob not to forget that they had a long drive to take him back to school the next day and Jacob said of course he hadn't forgotten.

Pick us up at ten, Jacob's father said. We'll stop in Montrose for lunch.

Okay.

Is Angie coming?

Yeah.

Okay.

On his way to the Tanners' house Jacob stopped at Sentry and bought a bag of popcorn kernels that they could make in a pan on the stove because the Tanners were out of popcorn Angie said and also because she liked the way it made the house smell like a movie theater. He also bought some orange colored cheese powder in a shaker to put on the popcorn because that was how Angie liked her popcorn and even though it was too salty for Jacob's taste and it colored his fingers orange he didn't mind eating it.

When Jacob got to the Tanners' house it was late in the afternoon and there was a pickup truck in the driveway and it was parked askew with the front end of it on the grass. He didn't recognize the truck at first but when he parked his mother's car beside it and sat there looking at it the reality of it set in and it was Jacob's worst fear come to pass because the truck belonged to Dale Swenson.

Jacob got out of the car and he left the Sentry bag with the popcorn and cheesy salt on the passenger seat and he ran to the front door of the house which was unlocked and he went inside. He didn't see anyone in the living room or the kitchen or the dining room and he was breathing fast and his heart was pounding such that he could feel the pressure of it in his chest. He felt like he was going to pass out but he couldn't let himself do that so he stood in the foyer of the house bent at the waist and clutching his knees and breathing deep breaths to guard against it.

When he thought he was no longer in danger of passing out Jacob went to the closet near the front door where the coats and boots and other things for use outdoors were stored and he found the baseball bat that he had asked the Tanners to keep there for safety reasons. Jacob stood there holding the bat in his hands and listening and when he did he heard the ceiling creak overhead as if someone were moving on the floor upstairs. Jacob went to the stairs and he didn't know if he should call out to Angie or not because he thought that if her father was there it might not be good to announce his presence because this might cause him to lose the element of surprise. He ran up the stairs and he was able to do it quietly because the stairs were covered in carpeting as was the hallway upstairs which rendered his footsteps mute.

There was a bathroom at the end of the hall and from inside the bathroom Jacob could hear the sound of shoes sliding on the floor and there were shuffling and grunting noises as well so Jacob ran to the door and he was holding the bat in his hands and it was raised over his shoulder when he looked into the bathroom.

Dale Swenson was in the bathroom and he was on his stomach and supporting his weight with his hands on the floor and his pants were pulled down and they were fouled with mud and grease and Angie was underneath him and her pants were pulled down as well and Dale Swenson was pushing himself inside her and his boots were scraping against the floor and making marks on it as he did and Angie wasn't fighting or moving nor was she making any sound and her eyes were closed and when Jacob saw blood on the floor where her head was he knew that she was unconscious or maybe dead.

Jacob screamed and he raised the bat over his head and when Dale Swenson turned to find the source of the scream his face was contorted as if conflicted by the pleasure of what he was doing and the surprise of seeing Jacob there and seeing what he was about to do. Jacob brought down the baseball bat in the manner of a lumberjack bucking a log with an axe and the bat vibrated in his hands when it struck Dale Swenson's head and there was a cracking sound and whether the sound came from the bat cracking or from Dale's skull cracking Jacob didn't know but he didn't care. Dale's eyes rolled into his head and he made a hissing sound through his teeth and he let himself down onto his daughter who was still unconscious or dead and he let himself down slowly as if his bones ached with the effort. As he settled onto Angie's body Dale's jaw clenched and the veins and ligaments were showing through the skin of his neck and as Dale Swenson fell unconscious the veins and ligaments began to disappear and his body went limp and the hissing stopped and then he was silent.

Jacob rolled Dale Swenson onto the floor with his foot and as he did this he could hear air rushing into Angie's lungs as if the weight of her father's body had shortened her breath and Jacob thought this was a good thing. He checked her neck for a pulse and he found one and then he said thank you god and laid his head on her chest and started to cry.

He didn't cry or lay on her chest very long because Angie had an injury to her head that was bleeding so Jacob lifted her head a little and looked for it and he found it on the back side of her head and it was a cut and it was swollen around the cut and it looked like her head may have struck something. Jacob looked up and saw that the edge of the sink was smeared with blood.

He looked at the injury to Angie's head again and it didn't seem to be bleeding much anymore. Jacob cleaned the wound with a washcloth and when he was done the washcloth was pink with blood so he put this in the sink and then he pulled up Angie's underwear and her pants and then he picked her up and carried her to the bedroom and put her on the bed. He went to the bathroom and found another washcloth and this one he left dry and he folded it into a square and placed it under Angie's head where her injury was and then he sat on the edge of the bed and watched her breathe.

There were tears on Angie's face that she had cried before she was unconscious and they had run down her cheek and some of the tracks that they had made were still wet but others were dry and just shadows of the tears that had made them. As he sat next to Angie on the bed watching her breathe Jacob thought about what to do with her father in the bathroom and he thought that if Dale wasn't already dead he wanted to finish the job with the baseball bat but then he stopped thinking about Dale because there would be time to think about what to do with him later. Right now he wanted Angie to wake up so that he could make sure she was all right but when he thought about it he wasn't sure if he wanted her to wake up or not because of how upset she would be and Jacob didn't want her to go through that. The more he thought about what her father had done to her not just in the bathroom of the Tanner house but for all of Angie's life the more angry Jacob became and because Angie wasn't waking up yet he decided to check on Dale Swenson and maybe an idea of what to do with him would come.

He went to the bathroom and the baseball bat was still on the floor where he had left it after hitting Dale with it and he picked it up and looked at it. There was no blood or hair or tissue on it and it looked like new so Jacob looked at Dale's head where he had struck him with the bat and there was a lump and a bruise there and even though the lump and the bruise were enormous and spread over the top of his head which was mostly bald there was no blood. Jacob thought this was a good thing but he really didn't know why he thought this because he didn't yet have any idea what he was going to do.

Dale was wearing a flannel shirt and it had the sleeves cut off of it which exposed his arms and shoulders and even though his arms were thin they were muscled and Jacob realized that Dale Swenson wasn't weak at all in fact he looked very strong. His pants and his underwear were still down around his ankles and he was on his side and his penis was still erect and when Jacob looked at it he became angrier than he had been before. He wanted to roll him over so he wouldn't have to look at it or maybe put a towel over it or cut it off with a butcher knife from the kitchen downstairs but in the end he didn't do any of these things and he left Dale on the floor as he was. Jacob checked the pockets of Dale's jeans for a knife or a gun or any other kind of weapon but he didn't find any so he watched him for a while and he hated to do it because he didn't want to look at him any longer than he had to but after a while he decided that Dale was still alive because he was still breathing even though it was shallow and weak.

Jacob thought that he should get Dale's truck out of the driveway to guard against someone seeing it there and getting involved in the situation. He thought that hiding the truck could be a bad thing and make them look guilty of something depending on what he and Angie decided to do but in the end he decided to do it anyway and he checked the pockets of Dale's jeans looking for the key to the truck but he couldn't find it. He went to the bedroom and looked at Angie on the bed and she was still unconscious so he put the bat on the floor by the bed and he went to Dale's truck which was still parked askew on the driveway. Jacob found the key in the ignition of the truck so he opened the garage door and drove the truck inside and then he got out of the truck and closed the garage door behind him. There was only one window to the outside in the garage and in front of it was a workbench so Jacob put some cardboard boxes that contained clothes and books and household items that had gone unsold in the town rummage sale onto the workbench to obscure the view through the window.

When he was done Jacob went outside and looked through the window to check his work and he couldn't see into the garage so he went back into the house. He could hear Angie in the bedroom as he was climbing the stairs and he heard her voice because she was talking to herself and when he got closer Jacob could hear that she was crying as well. She was still on the bed when Jacob entered the room and she was on her side looking away from the door and she had pulled her knees to her chest. Jacob sat on the bed and put his hand on her shoulder and when he did this Angie screamed and turned over on the bed and she was punching and kicking him as he sat there and she was cursing at him and telling him to rot in hell.

It's me, Jacob said.

Angie stopped kicking and punching him but she was still

crying and she was looking at him from where she lay on the bed and her hair was matted to her face with tears and sweat. When she realized that it was Jacob on the bed next to her and not her father she rolled away from him and pulled her knees to her chest again and she was still crying. Jacob thought about how stupid it was to touch her like that and not tell her who was touching her before he did it.

It's okay now, he said.

Angie didn't say anything and Jacob thought about touching her shoulder again to comfort her but he didn't because he didn't think there was much of anything he could do or say in the current situation that would be comforting but after a while she stopped crying.

Where is he, she said.

Angie was facing the other side of the room and Jacob couldn't see her face but her voice sounded calm when she said this.

In the bathroom.

What happened?

I hit him with the baseball bat.

Is he dead?

No.

Good.

What?

Angie rolled over and sat up on the edge of the bed next to Jacob and dried the tears on her face with the sleeve of her shirt. She cringed a little when she touched the injury on the back of her head but when she looked at the fingers she had used to touch it there wasn't any fresh blood on them.

Good, Angie said. I said that's good.

Jacob thought about this and realized that Angie had a plan or at least the beginnings of a plan for what to do with her father and he thought this was a good thing because he didn't have one.

Are you okay, Jacob said.

No I'm not okay.

You could have a concussion.

I don't have a concussion.

How do you know?

I just know.

Are you hurt anywhere else?

Of course I am.

Maybe you should see a doctor.

No I shouldn't.

Why not?

Angie looked at Jacob as if to tell him to stop being so stupid.

I know when I should see a doctor and when I shouldn't, she said.

Jacob said of course she would know that and he said that he was sorry for suggesting she wouldn't. Then he asked her why it was good that her father wasn't dead. Angie said that it was good that her father wasn't dead because she was going to kill him herself but first she was going to tell him how they killed his son Mark and buried him in a pit with rotting pigs.

When he heard this Jacob didn't know what to say and they sat there on the bed for some time not talking just sitting and thinking and when Angie had thought about things long enough she said that she was going to do it and she rose from the bed.

How are you going to do it, Jacob said.

I don't know.

You might not have to.

What?

He might just die anyway. I hit him pretty hard.

Well then I'd better hurry.

Angie smoothed the wrinkles in her shirt and her pants with her hand and then she looked in the mirror that was on the back of Mrs. Tanner's dresser and picked up a brush that was on the dresser and she brushed her hair. Jacob didn't know why Angie would be concerned about her appearance at a time like this and he thought that if she was going to kill her father she would want him to see what he had done to her before he died but then he thought that maybe she wouldn't want him to see that and maybe take some kind of pleasure from it. Then he thought that it might not matter at all what Angie looked like because Dale Swenson might be dead already. Angie looked at the baseball bat that Jacob had put on the floor by the bed for a little while and then she picked it up and went to the bedroom door and she turned and asked Jacob if he was coming.

Okay, Jacob said.

Dale had come to and he was still on the floor and his pants were around his knees and he was trying to pull them up but his grip on them would fail when he did. They would slip from his fingers and then he would try again and they would slip again and he was talking to himself in a whisper while he did this and he was looking at his pants as he tried to pull them up so he didn't see Angie and Jacob by the door until Angie called out to him.

Dale stopped trying to pull up his pants and he looked at Angie and at Jacob standing over him and he became angry and he tried to sit up but when he did the strength in his arms failed and he fell onto his side again.

The fuck you lookin at, Dale said.

Angie and Jacob didn't say or do anything and then Dale made a noise in his throat like the growl of an animal and he cursed them both. He tried to pull his pants up again and he groaned with the effort and he was able to lift them over his knees but before he could cover himself Angie raised the bat over her head and swung it down onto Dale's arm and broke it at the elbow against the floor. Dale screamed and cursed with the pain of his broken arm and with the pain in his head and he held his arm that wasn't broken over the top of his head and squeezed it to relieve the pain.

Angie stood over her father and she looked at him and she was holding the bat at her side and she watched him curse and scream with pain as he rolled on the floor of the Tanners' bathroom with his pants and underwear pulled down over his knees.

Jacob looked at Angie but he didn't say anything to her and he went to where the toilet was and he put the lid down and sat. He didn't know what she was going to do and he was nervous about what was going to happen but he didn't try to stop her because he thought she had the right to do whatever she wanted to him so he just sat and watched.

After some time Dale Swenson stopped screaming and cursing and he lowered his arm from his head and he looked up at Angie who was still standing over him and she was still holding the baseball bat at her side.

What're you gonna do, Dale said.

Angie didn't say anything for some time and as she stood

there looking at her father on the floor the baseball bat slipped from her hand and clattered and rolled on the floor and then Angie started to tremble and then she started to cry.

I don't know, she said.

Jacob went to where the bat had fallen on the floor and he kicked it away and he stood between Angie and her father and he took her hands and told her that things would be all right now because there was no one left who would hurt her anymore.

Angie didn't say anything to this and then Jacob looked at Dale and saw that he was on his elbow now and he was groaning with the effort of lifting his own weight and breathing heavily at the pain in his arm and the pain in his head but he was able to lift himself enough to sit on the floor. Angie was still crying and Jacob told her that he was going to take her to the bedroom again but Angie said no and sat against the wall facing her father and then she looked across the room at her father and her father looked at her as they sat on the floor of the Tanners' bathroom.

When she had stopped crying Angie looked at Jacob and her voice was still shaking a little when she spoke.

I can't do it, she said.

What'd you say, Dale said.

Jacob told Dale to shut up because no one was talking to him and then he sat on the floor next to Angie.

I didn't think you could, Jacob said.

I wanted to though, Angie said.

I know.

Nobody would miss him.

No they wouldn't.

Nobody would care.

No.

I wouldn't care, Angie said.

I guess you wouldn't.

Then why can't I do it?

Jacob thought about this and said that he guessed when it came down to it not missing someone when they're dead or not caring that they died in the first place is a lot different than killing someone. Angie didn't say anything and they looked at her father who was backing himself against the wall on the other side of the room by pushing with the heels of his boots and pulling against the sink with one hand and he was sliding on the linoleum because he had somehow been able to pull his pants up while Jacob and Angie were talking.

It's a hell of a thing to kill someone, Jacob said.

What're we going to do, Angie said.

I don't know. Until now I was following your plan.

I guess we need a new plan.

I guess we do.

They sat and watched Dale Swenson on the other side of the room and Dale was talking to himself and his arm that was broken was shaking and it lay on the floor next to him. Dale looked at his arm for a while and then he looked at Angie and he licked his lips and opened his mouth like he was going to say something to her but he didn't. He looked away instead and his whole body was shaking now and his eyes were wide and his nose was bleeding as well and he turned his head in every direction to look around the room as if he were surrounded by ghosts.

He's going to die isn't he, Angie said.

I think so.

Angie wiped the tears from her face and she turned to

Jacob and he took her in his arms and they sat there in the Tanners' bathroom with her dying father and it was the same bathroom where Angie and Megan Tanner had dressed and put on their makeup for prom.

Should I tell him, Angie said.

Jacob was still holding her and he looked at Dale over Angie's shoulder and he saw that the arm that wasn't broken was shaking now as were his legs and Dale had fallen almost to the floor on his side from lack of balance and his breathing was labored. Jacob thought that there wasn't a lot of time to say anything to him and even if they did tell Dale about killing Mark and burying him in Mr. Foster's pit he might not hear them or understand what they were saying.

It's up to you, Jacob said.

I don't think I want to.

Okay.

They didn't say anything for a long time they just sat there holding each other and not looking at Angie's father but they were listening to him breathing and Dale was whispering but the whispering wasn't directed at anyone it was just general whispering and after a while the whispering stopped and then the breathing stopped and they looked at him.

Is he dead, Angie said.

Jacob got up and went to where Dale Swenson lay on his side and he checked the pulse on his neck like he had done with Angie's brother Mark and there was no pulse so he told her that yes he was dead. Angie went to where Jacob and her father were and she sat on her heels and took Jacob's hand and they looked at her father who was dead on the floor.

Where do you think he is now, Angie said.

I don't know, Jacob said.

He's probably in hell.

I don't know.

He could be in heaven.

He's not in heaven.

He might have found Jesus, Angie said.

Even so, Jacob said.

Where do you think he is then?

Maybe he's nowhere.

What do you mean nowhere?

I mean nowhere.

How can someone just be nowhere?

Maybe that's how it works.

Do you really think that?

I don't know what I think.

They sat looking at Angie's father and his eyes were still open in death and they were cloudy and Jacob looked at them and he thought about closing them but then he decided not to. He looked at Angie and she was looking at the arm she had broken with the baseball bat and when she was done looking at his arm she looked at Jacob.

I was so stupid, she said.

What?

He wasn't weak.

You're not stupid.

Yes I am.

No you're not, Jacob said. It's okay.

No it isn't.

It will be.

Okay.

Jacob thought about what they should do with Dale Swenson's body and then he thought about what they had done with Mark's body and how they had gotten away with it. He thought about hiding the body of Dale Swenson like they did with the body of his son Mark but the more he thought about it the more he thought that the situation was different now and that there was really no reason to hide it because there was no one they had to protect themselves from anymore.

What should we do, Angie said.

I think we should call the sheriff.

Why?

People should know what he did.

They already know what he did.

I mean this.

Angie had been looking at her father while they were talking but now she looked at Jacob and there was a look of confusion or disbelief on her face like Jacob was in violation of some kind of understanding.

I don't want people to know about this, Angie said.

Jacob thought about this and realized that he was being insensitive about the situation because he didn't know what it was like from Angie's perspective and he didn't know how embarrassed he would be or whether he would want to go on living or just crawl into a hole and die. He thought that Angie should be able to decide what to do about their current situation because even though he was the one who killed Dale Swenson with a baseball bat she was the one who had been raped by her father.

Okay, Jacob said. I'm sorry.

Don't be sorry.

The doorbell rang and someone was knocking on the front door and Jacob and Angie gave a start and looked at each other and Jacob was scared and he could see by the expression on Angie's face that she was scared as well. The knocking was faint because they were so far away from it but Jacob could tell that whoever was at the door was knocking firmly on it.

Oh shit, Angie said. What do we do?

I don't know.

Shit.

Was someone coming over, Jacob said.

No.

Jacob rose from the floor and he was trembling with fear but he was also thinking of what to do.

Okay, he said. I'll see who it is and tell them you're sick or something.

Angie nodded and said okay.

Jacob went to the top of the stairs and stood there and wiped away the sweat that was on his forehead with his shirt sleeve and he ducked his head to see if he could see the front door from where he stood but he couldn't. The doorbell rang again and there was more knocking and this made Jacob start again. He looked down the hall and Angie was coming out of the bathroom and she looked at him and he looked back at her and then Angie closed the bathroom door behind her and went into the bedroom. Jacob went downstairs and unlocked the front door and opened it and Sheriff Grady was on the other side and he touched the brim of his hat and said hello Jacob.

Sheriff, Jacob said.

Everything okay here?

Jacob's stomach tightened with fear and his forehead felt

hot and he felt like he was going to throw up and he was worried that he was going to say something to the Sheriff that sounded suspicious or that he would say it in a way that looked suspicious and the more he worried about these things the more his stomach hurt and the hotter his forehead became. He shrugged his shoulders and said that things were okay for the most part but that Angie wasn't feeling well.

Is that your car outside?

Yeah.

The Tanners still out of town?

Yeah.

It's just the two of you at home then?

Yeah. What's the problem Sheriff?

Was Dale Swenson here this afternoon Jacob?

What?

Dale Swenson. Angie's father. Was he here?

No he wasn't here.

We got a report of his truck being parked in the Tanners' driveway. Did you see him?

Jacob was starting to sweat again and his hands were shaking from nerves and he thought about what would happen to him and to Angie if Sheriff Grady found out about Dale's body on the floor upstairs and then put the pieces together and figured out that he had killed Mark Swenson as well and disposed of the body in Mr. Foster's pit. Jacob didn't say anything for a long time and the Sheriff asked him again if Angie's father Dale Swenson had been at the Tanners' house that afternoon.

I don't know, Jacob said.

You don't know?

What?

You don't know if you saw him or not? Is that what you're saying?

Yeah.

The Sheriff heaved a sigh and then he looked past Jacob and into the house.

I'd like to speak with Angie, Sheriff Grady said. Is she upstairs?

Yeah but I think she's asleep.

Sheriff Grady looked at Jacob.

Jacob, he said. Someone may have seen Dale Swenson's truck parked outside this house. Why are you not alarmed by this?

Jacob nodded and said of course it was alarming and that he was sorry but he wasn't feeling too well himself. He invited Sheriff Grady into the house and told him that he would be right back with Angie but before Jacob could go upstairs Angie was already coming down and she was holding a tissue in her hand and it was crumpled and her hair was freshly tangled and her eyes were red from crying.

Sheriff, she said.

Sheriff Grady took off his hat and approached her and asked if she was all right and when he did Angie's face crumpled a little and she shook her head. Sheriff Grady motioned to the couch and told her to sit and then he looked at Jacob.

What happened here Jacob?

Jacob looked at Angie and she was blotting her eyes with the tissue and she was looking at the floor and he thought that the best thing to do now would be to tell the truth about what happened before things went too far and he would just have to come up with some kind of explanation for putting Dale's truck in the garage but before he could say anything Angie spoke.

He was here Sheriff, she said.

When Angie said this Jacob knew that she had a plan and he felt relieved that he wouldn't have to explain the presence of Dale Swenson's truck in the Tanners' garage but he didn't know how he felt about lying to Sheriff Grady nor did he know how he felt about Angie lying to the sheriff.

Your father was here, Sheriff Grady said.

Yes.

Did he hurt you?

No.

Okay, Sheriff Grady said. What happened?

He said he was sorry, Angie said.

He was sorry, Sheriff Grady said.

Yeah.

About what?

About everything.

What does that mean everything?

It means he was sorry for everything. The drinking and the beatings and for letting Mark do whatever he wanted to me and for doing it himself.

And what did you say?

I said I didn't believe him. I told him he wasn't sorry and that he was never going to change and to get the hell away from me.

Had he been drinking?

Yeah.

Okay. What happened when you told him to leave?

He got mad and said who the hell was I to talk to him like that and said I was nothing but a worthless whore.

It was getting hard for Angie to speak because of her emotions and she didn't say anything for a while and Sheriff Grady let her collect herself and she blotted her eyes with the tissue.

I'm sorry to have to ask you about all this, Sheriff Grady said.

It's okay, Angie said.

What happened after that?

Angie blew her nose into the tissue and then she folded it and put it on the couch next to her. She looked at Jacob and to Jacob it looked like she was trying to smile at him but she didn't.

He pushed me into the house and then he came inside and closed the door and pushed me again and I fell on the floor.

But you aren't hurt?

No I'm not hurt.

Okay.

He started to take his pants down, Angie said. He said he was going to teach me some respect and that's when Jacob came.

Sheriff Grady looked at Jacob and asked him why he said he didn't know if he saw Dale Swenson at the house or not.

I told him not to say anything to anyone sheriff, Angie said. Please don't be mad at Jacob.

Sheriff Grady looked at Angie and said that he just wanted to get to the truth about what happened and that he understood that she was embarrassed about what her father did to her and then he said he understood why Jacob would want to protect her.

Okay, Angie said.

Sheriff Grady asked Jacob what happened when he came into the house and Jacob said that Dale had thrown Angie onto the floor and it looked like he was going to hurt her or rape her or both so he came up behind Dale and put his arm around his neck in a choke hold and pulled him outside and threw him down the porch steps and onto the lawn. Jacob said that after he threw Dale out of the house he told him to go home and if he ever came back he would kill him and no one would care not even the sheriff because everyone knew there was a court order telling him to stay away from Angie and they would all say he had it coming. He said that Dale had some trouble getting up from the ground on account of his pants still being down and because of his age but eventually he did get up and then he pulled up his pants and got into his truck and left.

Did he say anything to you Jacob, Sheriff Grady said.

No.

Did you see which way he went?

No I was concerned about Angie at that point.

Okay.

Sheriff Grady asked Angie if her father had been to the Tanners' house before or if he had tried to contact her or threaten her before this and Angie said no and that this was the first time he had been in violation of the court order. Then the sheriff asked her if there was any reason she knew of that her father would come today to try and hurt her and Angie said that no she couldn't think of anything.

What happens now, Jacob said.

Well I need to get Dale's side of the story, Sheriff Grady said. But from the looks of it he'll be locked up for a while.

Okay, Jacob said.

I'll check his house again and Bluff Road. See if I can scare him up.

Okay.

Are you kids okay? I could put a deputy outside until we find him. If it would be of some comfort to you.

Jacob looked at Angie and she looked at Jacob and they both shook their heads and Jacob told the sheriff thank you but it wouldn't be necessary because he wouldn't be leaving Angie alone anymore. He said that they were going to lock the doors and find Kyle Tanner's baseball bat and watch a movie and then the next morning Angie was coming with his family to take him back to college and that by the time she returned in the afternoon the Tanners would be home. When Jacob said this Sheriff Grady said that maybe they should spend the night with Jacob's parents for extra security and this would kill two birds with one stone he said since they needed to tell Jacob's parents about what happened with Dale anyway. Jacob and Angie looked at each other again and Angie shrugged and Jacob couldn't think of any reason why this would be a bad idea so he shrugged as well and told the sheriff that going to his house was a good idea and they would do it.

Good, Sheriff Grady said. And I'll let you two know as soon as we find him.

Okay, Angie said. Thank you sheriff.

Not at all, Sheriff Grady said. Take care Angie.

Angie went upstairs to clean herself up she said and to pack some things for the night and Jacob and the sheriff went outside and went to the sheriff's car which was parked next to the car that belonged to Jacob's mother. The sheriff's car was parked near the place where Dale Swenson's truck had been and the sheriff stood there looking at the tracks left in the grass by the front tires of the truck and he asked Jacob about them and Jacob confirmed to the sheriff that Dale was parked askew in the driveway and that his truck had made the tracks. Sheriff Grady looked at them for some time not saying anything just studying them and he looked down the driveway and at the road as if piecing together what had occurred and then he looked at the garage. Jacob started to feel nervous again and he thought for sure that the sheriff would look in the garage and figure out what really happened but he didn't and instead the sheriff said that he was glad Jacob had come when he did and that Angie was fortunate to have him as a friend to which Jacob replied that he was fortunate to have Angie as a friend as well.

Of course, Sheriff Grady said.

Thanks sheriff.

I have to say Dale Swenson is fortunate as well.

What?

To be alive, Sheriff Grady said.

Jacob didn't say anything.

If I'd have come in and seen that I might have killed him right there. Lawman or not.

I wanted to sheriff.

I imagine you did.

Don't know why I didn't.

No one can say what they'd do in a situation until it comes I guess.

That sounds right.

I'll be in touch Jacob.

Okay.

Sheriff Grady got into his car and backed down the Tanners' driveway and onto the road and drove away and Jacob waited in the driveway for a little while in case the sheriff came back but he didn't so Jacob went into the house and locked the door and went upstairs. Angie was standing in the doorway of the bathroom and her arms were crossed in front of her and she was looking at her father who was still dead on the floor by the sink and he was still lying on his side with his eyes open.

Are you okay, Jacob said.

I don't know, Angie said.

They went to the bedroom and they sat together on the bed and they didn't say anything for a long time. Jacob thought about what they should do now and he was out of ideas of what to do with dead people because Mr. Foster's pit was sealed with dirt and grown over with brush and there was nowhere else he could think of to put Dale Swenson. Even though he didn't know what to do he didn't care because Angie was safe and they didn't have to worry anymore about her father or her brother or anyone. He thought that no matter what they decided to do now it would be the right thing because they were the only ones who understood the situation they were in and there was no wrong thing to do if they did it together.

Is it true what you told the sheriff, Jacob said.

Is what true?

That he came to say he was sorry.

It's true.

Jacob didn't say anything to this and he thought that inside of everyone no matter how bad they are there is probably some good and maybe Dale Swenson found the good inside himself even though it was too late. Then he started thinking again about what they should do about Angie's dead father in the bathroom and he thought about how they would have to do something with not only Dale's body but his truck as well and

Jacob knew there wasn't a lot of time to do it because they had to leave the Tanners' house and go to his house soon because the sheriff was probably going to check on them later.

As Jacob thought about these things he was getting nervous again but then Angie looked at Jacob and said I know what to do.

What, Jacob said.

Are you going to do it with me, Angie said.

Of course I am.

No matter what?

No matter what.

Okay.

* * *

Jacob parked his mother's car on the gravel next to Dale Swenson's house and he turned off the engine and the headlights as well and he and Angie sat there for a while not saying anything or moving just listening and the windows in the car were down but the only thing they could hear was the sound of crickets in the field. It was getting dark but there was still enough light to see the corn that was standing in Dale Swenson's field. It had been planted in the spring of the year that Mark Swenson disappeared and it hadn't been harvested nor chopped since then but just left to rot where it stood and most of the stalks were broken and bent to the ground and among the stalks grew thistle and weeds.

They got out of the car and Angie went to the front porch of the house and the boards creaked under her feet as she walked on the porch and at the end of the porch was a lawn chair and it was of the kind made of plastic webbing wrapped around hollow tubes of aluminum. The webbing on the chair was dirty and it was frayed and torn in places and the tubing was misshapen at the joints which made them squeak when Angie collapsed it for storage. She gave the chair to Jacob and then tried the front door and when she did it was unlocked so she opened the door and went inside and turned to look at Jacob.

I'll be right back, she said.

Okay, Jacob said.

Angie closed the door behind her and Jacob went to the car and opened the trunk and he put the chair inside and then he closed the trunk and leaned against the side of the car and watched the house. He didn't know if the sheriff had already been inside looking for Dale or not but he thought that the sheriff would probably come to the house every now and then until he found him so Jacob was nervous.

He thought about the day that he buried Mark Swenson under the pigs in Mr. Foster's pit and about how he wasn't very nervous at all that day. Jacob figured he wasn't nervous because he knew that what they were doing was the right thing to do and that it was the best way to protect Angie and himself from Dale Swenson which was something he couldn't say in their current situation. He also thought that because he was infatuated with Angie then and because he thought about her all the time that he would have done anything to impress her and protect her and make her happy and prove his feelings for her. He thought about this and thought that maybe things were different now not because he didn't care about her or that he wouldn't do everything to protect her but because he was less emotional about things now and thought more reasonably about things. Then he thought about the plan that Angie had formulated on the

Tanners' bed and he thought about how it wasn't a good plan and that he only agreed to it because he felt bad about what Dale had done to her. Jacob thought that he shouldn't have hidden Dale's truck in the garage nor should they have lied to the sheriff about what happened and he also thought that Angie shouldn't have worried so much about what people would find out or what they would think or say because after all none of it was her fault and everyone would know it. The more he thought about these things and about what they were doing the more he thought they were making a big mistake and that they shouldn't be doing it because it was wrong and that they should have told the truth about what happened to Sheriff Grady.

    Angie came out of the house and she was carrying a bottle of whiskey that was mostly empty and she was also carrying a flashlight and a pair of binoculars and the strap of the binoculars was broken. She closed the door and walked across the porch that squeaked and the strap of the binoculars swung in the air as she walked.

    Let's go, she said.

    Okay, Jacob said.

    Angie put the whiskey and the flashlight and the binoculars on the floor of the car on the passenger side and she and Jacob got into the car and Jacob backed it onto the road and they drove away.

    Did anyone drive by the house, Angie said.

    No.

    Good.

    They didn't say anything else as they were driving and Jacob figured this was because they had probably said everything they needed to say and now they just needed to focus on doing what they agreed they were going to do.

Jacob turned onto Bluff Road and it was full dark now and the woods were devoid of light from the moon or from street lamps or from any other source and when they drove into the picnic area there were no other vehicles there just a truck that was always parked there at night and it was for use by the park maintenance staff during normal work hours but now it just sat empty and idle.

Okay, Angie said. Let's go.

Jacob didn't say anything and he drove to the highway and back to the Tanner house and he pulled his mother's car up the driveway to the garage and turned off the engine but he didn't get out of the car he just sat there looking out the windshield and breathing.

Jacob, Angie said. Let's go.

Are you sure we should do this, Jacob said.

What?

It's probably not too late to tell the truth.

Yes it is.

I don't think it is.

What's going on Jacob?

I've just been thinking.

You said we'd do this together no matter what.

I know I did. I've just been thinking is all.

We can't stop now. This is the only way it'll work out.

Jacob didn't say anything.

What are you doing Jacob, she said. Don't do this.

Jacob looked at her and there was a little bit of light from the dashboard and it illuminated her features and her eyes were shining with tears and her face was colored blue from the dashboard lights and Jacob thought that her heart would break if he didn't go through with their plan but he also thought that his soul would probably be lost if they did go through with it.

I need you Jacob, Angie said.

Jacob didn't say anything for some time and then he shook his head and said okay.

He got out of the car and when he did Angie moved over to the driver's seat and she was wiping the tears from her face with her hands and when Jacob looked at her under the illumination of the dome light he could see by the expression on her face that she was upset and terrified and her hands were shaking and then she looked up at him.

I love you, she said.

Jacob closed the door of the car and lowered himself and kissed her through the open window.

I love you too, he said.

Angie had given Jacob the keys to the Tanner house so Jacob unlocked the side door of the garage and went inside and turned on the lights and returned the cardboard boxes of unsold rummage sale items to their original locations. He opened the overhead door and when he did Angie started the car and light came into the garage from the headlights and Jacob used the light to look at the body of Dale Swenson in the back of the truck and it was concealed by a tarp he had found on a shelf next to Mr. Tanner's workbench. Jacob checked the edges of the tarp to make sure they were tucked under Dale's body and when he was satisfied he turned off the garage lights and got into the truck and started it and when he did Angie backed the car away to let Jacob out of the garage. Jacob backed the truck onto the driveway and then he got out and went into the garage and closed the overhead door and locked it and went out the side door and locked it behind him.

They drove back to Bluff Road and they followed the posted speed limits and they didn't drive too close together and they drove cautiously in all ways to keep from drawing attention to themselves or their vehicles. When they got to the picnic area Angie pulled the car to the side of the road and the road formed a loop that went around the parking lot and back to the highway and when Jacob caught up to her he pulled Dale Swenson's truck over as well and turned off the engine.

Jacob got out of the truck and closed the door and went to the back of the truck and lowered the tailgate. He held Dale Swenson by the ankles and pulled his body to the back of the truck and then he unwrapped him from the tarp and bundled up the tarp and put it on the ground. Angie was holding the flashlight and she was using it to guide herself to the back of the truck and the lawn chair was hooked in her arm and she was holding the bottle of whiskey and the binoculars as well and when she came to where Jacob was she illuminated Dale's body in the bed of the truck. Jacob turned Dale onto his stomach and pulled him out until his legs were hanging from the back of the truck and then he turned and lowered himself under Dale's body and lifted him onto his shoulder and walked into the woods.

Jacob heard the sound of Angie closing the tailgate of the truck behind him and then the ground in front of him was illuminated by the flashlight and the light bounced in the duff and the undergrowth because Angie was running to catch up to him.

To the right, Angie said.

Jacob turned to the right and the light on the ground before him turned as well and after they had walked a short distance through the woods the light was swallowed by the darkness at a clearing in the undergrowth and at the edge of the undergrowth the ground turned to stone and Jacob stopped walking because he knew they had come to the edge of Indian Bluff and then he lowered himself to one knee and put Dale Swenson on the ground.

When she reached the place where Jacob was Angie put the whiskey and the binoculars on the ground and then she unfolded the lawn chair and positioned it at the edge of the undergrowth and she was using the flashlight to guard against falling from the bluff. She picked up the bottle of whiskey and rubbed it down with her shirt sleeve and took off the cap and dropped the cap and the bottle onto the ground next to the chair and some of the whiskey spilled from the bottle as it lay there and in the illumination from the flashlight Jacob watched as the whiskey ran across the rocky ground and over the edge of the bluff. Jacob looked over the side of the bluff and there was a fire on the beach and there were people standing around it and he stepped closer to the edge to get a better look and to see if there was anyone closer to the bottom of the bluff but he couldn't see anything because the trees below concealed the ground there.

There's some people down there, Jacob said.

I know, Angie said. It'll be okay.

Be careful with that light.

Okay.

Angie picked up the binoculars and rubbed them down with her sleeve as well and then she put them on the lawn chair and she aimed the light at the ground as she did this to keep from alerting the people on the beach to their presence. When she was done with this she looked at Jacob and she was pointing the flashlight at the ground and both she and Jacob were illuminated by the reflection of its light off the rock at the edge of the bluff.

Are you ready, she said.

Yeah.

Angie put the flashlight on the lawn chair and aimed its light at the back of the chair and the light reflected by the plastic webbing was enough to guide them and they picked up Dale Swenson each of them to an end with Jacob at his head and Angie at his feet and they carried him to the edge of the bluff.

On three, Angie said.

Okay.

They swung Dale's body in the air like a hammock and Angie used the rhythm of the swinging to count to three and as she did Jacob's legs began to wobble and he felt like he was going to throw up and his arms and hands felt weak and he thought his grip under Dale's armpits would give out before Angie reached three and he felt like he was going to pass out but he didn't and when Angie said three they let go and threw Dale Swenson over the edge.

Jacob fell to his knees and he put his hands on the ground to support his weight and his head was spinning and his ears were hot and there was no sound and it was like he was underwater and to Jacob it felt like the world had stopped turning and he had been left behind on its cold and dead surface but then there was sound again and it was the sound of the dead and dried leaves of autumn rustling and falling from the trees in the dark and it was the sound of branches groaning and breaking with stress and it was the sound of Dale Swenson striking the rocks below and when he heard these sounds Jacob sat on his heels and he was shaking with grief and he said oh god oh god and the world was still spinning and there was no light only movement and falling and sickness and despair and there was the sound of Dale Swenson calling from the rocks below I'm sorry I'm sorry and then there was nothing only darkness.

* * *

In the darkness came a dream but it was a memory as well and in the dream Jacob was ten years old and he was fishing with his father from the boat and they were on Indian Lake. They were fishing for pike because it was fall and the lake was calm like glass and there was fog on the water because it was early but there was enough light to see the colors of the leaves through the fog. They were trolling the depths of the lake and Jacob was steering their course with the electric motor and in addition to steering the boat he was watching his pole which was set across the gunnels and the tip of his pole was vibrating from the movement of the lure he was using. In the water behind the boat was a pike on a stringer and it rolled and bubbled in the wake of the boat and it was almost dead and only now and then would it thrash its tail to attempt escape and when it did Jacob would look at it. His hands were cold from holding the handle of the electric motor and also from bracing his pole against his knees to keep it from falling off the gunnels. To warm his hands he would put them in the water and drag them beside the boat because the water was warmer than the air but when he did this he could only warm one of his hands at a time because he needed to maintain control over the boat with the other hand and the warmth was only temporary because when he took his hand out of the water it would cool quickly due to the coldness of the air.

Do you think we'll get another one dad, Jacob said.

I think so, Jacob's father said.

And then we'll have enough for supper?

Yes we will.

The pike on the stringer thrashed on the surface of the lake and the empty clips on the stringer rattled and then the pike tried to swim under the boat but it couldn't because it was too weak and the boat was moving too fast so it stopped trying and then it was rolling in the wake again and Jacob watched as all of this happened.

Does it make you sad, Jacob said.

Does what make me sad.

To kill the fish.

No it doesn't make me sad.

It makes me a little sad.

Jacob's father turned and looked at Jacob and told him that in the circle of things the pike were supposed to be food for people and sometimes for other animals as well just like the smaller fish were supposed to be food for the pike. He said that this was the way things worked and the pike weren't sad about killing and eating the smaller fish and the other animals that killed and ate the pike weren't sad so there was no reason for Jacob to be sad either.

But fish and animals don't think like us, Jacob said.

I guess they don't.

And they have to eat other animals or they'll die.

We have to eat too.

We could eat other stuff.

Do you want to let the pike go?

Jacob thought about this and said that he didn't want to

let the pike go he was just a little sad about killing it.

You'll probably feel differently about it when you're older, Jacob's father said.

Like you do?

Yes like I do.

Is that why you're a hero?

What?

You're a hero right?

No I'm not a hero.

Grandpa said you are.

Jacob's father didn't say anything.

He said you were a hero for being in the war.

That doesn't make me a hero.

He said you saved your friend from getting killed.

A lot of people did that.

He said you had to kill someone else to do it. Because they were going to kill your friend.

Jacob's father put his fishing pole down on the floor of the boat and turned around in his seat and looked at Jacob and told him that yes he did kill someone to save his friend but that the next day his friend died when a bomb exploded under his vehicle so he really didn't know if he accomplished anything by killing the guy that he killed because his friend was going to die anyway. He also said that he only killed that one person in the entire war because he wasn't there to kill people he was there to help people and he said that the people that were there to kill people had to kill a lot more people than he did.

Did it make you sad to kill someone, Jacob said.

Jacob's father looked away from Jacob and he shook his head and he looked at the lake and the fog that was there and he did this for some time before he looked at Jacob again.

Not when I did it.

Because you had to.

Because I had to.

Were you sad about it later?

Yes.

Are you still sad about it?

Yes I am. Sometimes even more sad than I am about my friend that died.

Because it was you that did it.

Right.

And because killing people is different than killing animals or pike.

Yes.

Even if they're bad?

It's a hell of a thing to kill someone Jacob. Even if they're bad.

Okay.

It doesn't make you a hero, Jacob's father said.

Okay.

Jacob's father said that some guys in the war killed a lot of people and for some of them it was more people than they could count and they weren't sad about doing it either because when they were doing it they were trying to save their own lives or the lives of their friends but when the killing was done and they came home to their families and their friends and their jobs they would get sad and they were much sadder than me.

Are they heroes, Jacob said.

Yes they are, Jacob's father said.

But not because they killed people.

No not because of that.

I don't think I know what a hero is anymore.

No one does Jacob.

I hope I never have to kill someone.

I hope not.

PART 3

Broken Tusks

Six Years Later

JACOB drove Mr. Foster's four wheeler down the trail from the stand and he drove slowly to keep from damaging the trailer that was hitched to it and when he got to the gravel road he parked next to his father's truck and turned off the engine. Jacob and his father got into the trailer and lifted the deer that was inside of it into the back of the truck and they lifted it by the legs each of them to an end and it was an eight pointer and even though it was dressed out it was still heavy and Jacob's father struggled to lift his end over the side of the truck. When they were done putting the deer into the truck they looked at each other and Jacob's father was breathing heavily and they were both smiling because it was the first deer Jacob had killed with a bow and they were both still excited about that.

They put their bows and their duffels and the other gear they had used in the stand into the truck with the deer and when they had everything unloaded from the trailer they climbed out of it and stood by the front of the truck.

You sure you don't want to come for supper, Jacob's father said.

Tomorrow, Jacob said. And if Bill doesn't show up tonight don't go trying to hang this deer by yourself.

You got something to eat?

In my pack. Cheesy noodles.

What every growing boy needs.

I'll be fine. Did you hear what I said about hanging the

deer?

    I heard you.

    Okay. See you in the morning.

    Okay.

    Jacob's father got into his truck and started the engine and backed down the gravel drive to the main road because the drive was too narrow to turn the truck around and Jacob watched until his father was out of sight and then he got on the four wheeler and drove it up the trail and parked it under the stand. Jacob climbed into the stand and opened his backpack and inside the pack was a small bottle of vodka. He took out the bottle and unscrewed the cap and took a drink and screwed the cap back on the bottle and put the bottle in his pocket.

    Jacob climbed down the ladder and went to the field road and stood there looking at Mr. Foster's field and the corn had recently been harvested and on the ground were broken stalks and chaff and loose corn and as he stood there looking at the field Jacob took the bottle out of his pocket and took a drink. He thought about the deer he had shot with the bow and how it had been walking up the path from the gravel drive to feed here and Jacob smiled a little at the memory of how happy it had made his father. He didn't put the bottle back in his pocket he just stood there holding it and now he was looking at the place where the field road went into the woods and he thought about the day he shot Mark Swenson in the neck with his father's twelve gauge. He thought about how he buried him there and about how his bones were now mingled under the soil with those of Mr. Foster's pigs and those of the boars he shot and he thought about how he was only fourteen when he did these things.

    Jacob went to the place where Mark was buried and he

stood there looking at the stone he had placed over the location of Mark's body but the stone was only an estimation of the location because he had placed it there after Mr. Foster had sealed the pit with soil. He raised the bottle of vodka a little as if in a toast to Mark's memory but instead of toasting his memory Jacob said fuck you Mark Swenson. He told Mark Swenson under the stone that he should be burning in hell for what he did to him and to Angie and that it was his own fault that he was buried there forever with the bones of pigs.

God damn you, Jacob said.

Jacob took a drink and he was starting to get drunk and he poured a little bit of the vodka onto the stone and he watched as the stone darkened where the alcohol ran down its sides. At first Jacob thought this was a suitable way to remember Mark Swenson but the more he thought about it the more he thought that it wasn't suitable at all so he put the bottle in his pocket and then he urinated on the stone and when he was done he went back to the stand.

He sat on the four wheeler for some time not doing anything just sitting and thinking and holding the bottle of vodka in his hands and he would drink from it now and then and after a while Jacob got off the four wheeler and went down the path and across the gravel lane and into the woods on the other side to where the observation tower stood near the edge of the park. Jacob climbed the stairs of the tower and when he got to the top he was tired and breathing heavily and he sat on the bench and put the bottle on the bench next to him and he sat there looking at it. The bottle was almost empty and Jacob was very drunk now and when he looked at the bottle it turned in his vision and when he tried to stand up he became dizzy not only from the alcohol but from the effort of climbing the stairs of the tower and from the height as well.

He went to the edge of the tower and when he did he stumbled a little so he held onto the railing to guard against falling and he looked at Indian Bluff across the lake and he was looking for the place where he and Angie had thrown the body of Dale Swenson from the top of it but he couldn't find it because the world was turning in his vision from vertigo. He looked through the scope that was mounted to the railing and he looked at the bluff with that but this made him even more dizzy and when Jacob took his eyes away from the scope he fell backwards onto the floor of the tower and when he did he struck his head on the bench and then he rolled onto his side and threw up.

Jacob didn't get up from the floor nor did he want to so he lay on his side thinking about Dale Swenson and Mark Swenson and how they had ruined his life and how he never should have spoken to Angie Swenson by the bike racks on the last day of ninth grade. As he thought these things he was looking at the bluff and even though he was lying down and not moving the world was still turning and its turning grew faster and the world was tipped on its axis and Jacob reached for the railing to keep from sliding off the tower and he closed his eyes and cried out for the turning to stop but when he opened his eyes the world hadn't stopped turning and it was still tipped on its axis and then Jacob tried to cry out again but he was mute and then he closed his eyes against the turning once more and when he did he passed out.

* * *

A boar came out of the woods and it had come to eat loose corn that had fallen during the harvest and when it walked onto Mr. Foster's field it saw the four wheeler that was parked in the woods on the other side and it stopped. The boar stood there for some time not moving just looking across the field and smelling the air and turning its ears to listen and when it was done looking and smelling and listening it went across the field to where the four wheeler sat under the stand and the boar didn't stop to eat loose corn as it crossed the field and when it was next to the four wheeler the boar stopped. It stood there and it watched the trail to the gravel road and when it turned its ears again there was the sound of footsteps coming up the trail and the boar knew that they were human footsteps but it didn't spook it just stood there watching the trail and listening and waiting.

* * *

Jacob woke and he was still on his side on the floor of the observation tower and there was vomit pooled by his head where he lay and in fact it was the stink of vomit that had woken him. He rose from the floor and sat on the bench and he was slow in getting up because he was still a little drunk and he was dizzy and his head hurt from striking it on the bench. The vodka bottle was on the bench next to him and he held it up and looked at it and it was empty so he put it back down on the bench and then he rubbed the place on his head where it had struck the bench and he checked his hand for blood but there was none. He got up and went down the stairs of the tower and he left the bottle on the bench and even though littering was something his father had always told him not to do Jacob didn't think leaving a bottle on the bench of an observation tower was littering because the tower didn't really belong in the woods either and when you thought about it the tower itself could be called litter as well.

When Jacob returned to the stand it was late in the afternoon but there was still plenty of day left and because he was out of vodka he couldn't think of anything to do so he decided to wait until he wasn't drunk anymore and then he would take Mr. Foster's four wheeler to his mother and father's house for supper. He took the pin out of the trailer and unhitched it and put the pin back in the hitch and then he lowered the trailer to the ground on its tongue and when he was finished unhitching the trailer from the four wheeler he heard someone stirring in the stand above him.

Hello Jacob, Angie said.

Jacob looked up and Angie Swenson was looking at him over the wall of the stand and he knew it was Angie because her voice was the same as it always was but she looked different than he remembered her and in fact she looked so different that he might not have recognized her in a different situation.

Angie, he said.

They stood there for a long time looking at each other and not saying anything and Jacob didn't know what to say because he wasn't happy or sad to see her and he wasn't angry or not angry and he wasn't excited or nervous or surprised to see her he wasn't any of these things and he just stood there looking at her and he didn't feel one way or another about seeing her.

Do you want me to come down, she said.

No I'll come up.

Jacob climbed into the stand and he closed the hatch and sat next to Angie on the floor and he looked at her and her face was pale and sunken and her hair was cut close to her head and the skin of her hands was discolored like it was translucent and it was stretched tightly over the bones underneath so tightly that Jacob thought it might tear and as he looked at her he didn't think she was beautiful but neither did he think she wasn't.

    How are you Jacob, Angie said.

    A little drunk.

    I see that.

    You look different, Jacob said.

    You look different too.

    Jacob didn't say anything to this and he asked Angie if she smoked. She said that she did so Jacob took some cigarettes from his backpack and gave her one and he took one for himself as well and he lit them with the lighter that was inside the plastic wrapping of the pack and when their cigarettes were lit he put the lighter back in the wrapping and set everything on the floor between them.

    They sat in the stand smoking and looking at the opposite wall and not at each other and Jacob wondered what kind of drug Angie was taking and when he thought about it he decided that there was probably more than one kind of drug she was taking. He thought that she probably didn't have any money because of the condition of her clothes which were torn and soiled but with what they were soiled Jacob had no idea. He wondered if she sold herself for drugs and he wondered how many times she had done it and with what kind of people and he wondered what sort of disease she might have and Jacob thought that wondering about these things should have made him angry or sad but it didn't.

    Where did you go, Jacob said.

Different places.

What kind of places?

Mostly bad places.

I thought you were going to live with your uncle.

I was but then I didn't.

Jacob finished his cigarette and leaned forward and crushed it against the coffee can that sat on the floor of the stand for this purpose and when it was out he dropped the butt into the can and leaned back against the wall.

You could've come back, he said.

I could've.

But you didn't.

I thought about it.

But you didn't do it.

No I didn't.

You could've called, Jacob said.

Angie didn't say anything she just sat and smoked her cigarette and the ash fell into her lap but she didn't seem to mind and she smoked the cigarette down to the filter and when it had extinguished itself she threw the filter into the can and looked at Jacob.

I'm here now, she said.

Yes you are.

So that's something.

Jacob looked at her and said that yes it was something and he asked her what she was going to do now and Angie said she didn't know but that she would figure things out. Jacob didn't say anything and he looked at her hands and he saw something there so he looked closer and then he took her hand and turned it over and pushed up the sleeve of her jacket and on the inside of

Angie's wrist were scars and the scars went up the length of her wrists and they were of different sizes and colors as if they had been made at different times with different intentions and on her arm above the scars were tracks and needle marks and then Jacob pushed up the other sleeve of Angie's jacket and Angie didn't protest when he did and on that arm he saw scars and tracks and needle marks as well. When Jacob was done looking at Angie's arms he pulled the sleeves of her jacket down and he held her hands and looked at her but he didn't say anything.

    Don't look at me like that, Angie said.

    Like what?

    Like you are.

    I wasn't looking at you like anything.

    Then what are you doing?

    Thinking.

    Thinking what?

    That I want to kill myself too.

    Angie shook her head and looked away from Jacob and she was looking over the wall of the stand into the trees and the leaves were at their peak of color.

    No you don't, Angie said.

    Jacob said that he did want to kill himself and that he had thought about it a lot over the years and the only reason he hadn't done it yet was because his mother and father were still alive and he didn't want to put them through that. He said that he had made a promise to himself that when they died he would do it because then there would be no one left who would care if he did it or not.

    Angie looked at him and her eyes were wet with tears and she told him that what he said was bullshit because if someone really wanted to do it they would just do it and not care what anyone thought because all they would care about is getting rid of the pain. She said that when she cut herself on the wrists she hadn't really wanted to do it either because if she really wanted to be dead she would have done it right instead of just half assed like she did.

    Jacob thought about this for a while and said that she was probably right and that he really didn't know anything about anything except that he was sad all the time and that he thought about her brother Mark and her father Dale all the time and when he thought about them he got sad which didn't make any sense because he should be happy that they were gone because they were bad people and he should also be happy because he and Angie got away with everything they did but he wasn't happy and he hadn't been happy in a long time and all he ever wanted to do now was to get drunk.

    Angie looked at him and said that she felt the same way and she said that by leaving she thought she would forget about her brother and father and what they did to her and she thought she would forget about what she and Jacob had done and maybe in time she would forget about Jacob as well and she could start a new life but after a while she knew she could never forget any of those things and that she was stupid for thinking she could.

    You're not stupid, Jacob said.

    Well I'm something, Angie said.

    We're both something.

    What are we then?

    I don't know.

    We're both pretty fucked up, Angie said.

    Jacob smiled a little.

I guess that's what we are then, he said.

They each lit a cigarette and they sat there smoking and looking over the wall of the stand at the trees and the leaves on them had turned yellow and orange and red and when there was a breeze the leaves would fall around them and into the stand. Jacob thought about the deer he had shot over the wall with the bow and he thought about how happy that had made his father and then he thought about the boars he had shot with his father's twelve gauge when he was fourteen.

He took the necklace out of his shirt by its chain and it was the necklace made with the cross Angie had given him and the boar tusk he had cut from a boar's head with his father's backsaw and he looked at Angie and said that he was glad she came. Angie looked at Jacob and said she was glad as well and she took her necklace out of her shirt and the tusk on her necklace was of higher quality than Jacob's in both general appearance and workmanship and it was still strung with twine and she laid it on her chest and then she took Jacob's hand and put her head on his shoulder.

I saw a boar when I came, she said.

You saw a boar?

Yeah.

Where?

By the four wheeler.

Jacob thought about this and about how surprising it was that she saw a boar because he hadn't seen one in years and neither had his father or Mr. Foster and there had been no sign of boars anywhere in a long time not even in the fields.

Did it have a broken tusk, Jacob said.

What?

I said did it have a broken tusk.

I don't know, Angie said.

Jacob nodded and thought about his question and why he would ask it and he decided he had no idea what an answer to it would mean either yes or no. As he thought about this he and Angie sat together neither of them speaking and they watched the leaves stir and click against the walls of the stand as they fell from the trees.

Also by Brian J. Anderson

The Ascent of PJ Marshall
Ghosts of Florence Pass

For exclusive access to Brian J. Anderson's latest work in progress, along with information about author promotions, giveaways and contests, visit bjandersonauthor.com.

Made in the USA
San Bernardino, CA
07 September 2016